Don't Start Now

– MICHAEL LIMMER –

An environmentally friendly book
www.printondem

Mixed Sources
Product group from well-managed
forests, and other controlled source
www.fsc.org Cert no. TT-COC-0026
© 1996 Forest Stewardship Council

D1419766

www.fast-print.net/store.php

Don't Start Now
Copyright © Michael Limmer 2013

A catalogue record for this book is available from the British Library

ISBN 978-178035-589-4

First published 2013 by
FASTPRINT PUBLISHING
Peterborough, England.

I am: yet what I am none cares or knows,

My friends forsake me like a memory lost;

I am the self-consumer of my woes…

- John Clare

1

I found her photograph today. It slipped out from between the pages of a book I hadn't opened in years. I wish it had remained unopened.

I thought I'd lost that photograph years ago; as if I could ever lose the memory. I stooped and picked it up, stared into the face which even now is constantly snapping at the frontier of my dreams. I felt the old wounds reopening, and perhaps I shouldn't have been surprised.

Because none of them have ever healed.

★★★

Blore emerged from the shadow of the church into a biting wind as he followed the tortuous path towards the cemetery. October had already brought a couple of hard frosts, and the leaves had begun to wilt and rain down from the trees. Head down, he shuffled through them as they drifted across his path. The grey day was fitting both for his mood and outlook, as well as for the war-riddled century limping towards its close.

He came on to a wide tree-lined avenue and spotted a hearse at the end of it. Off to the right, a knot of mourners huddled round a grave. Drawing nearer, Blore picked out the minister's white surplice, heard the drone of familiar words: *"Ashes to ashes…"*

He paused, waiting at a respectful distance. The gathering stood with heads bowed, their faces grim on a dour day: mostly men, few under fifty. He guessed they'd be former colleagues, used to death and betraying little emotion.

The service over, the mourners dispersed, walking back up the avenue in twos and threes. Blore found the man he sought: he was walking alone. She'd told him he'd probably be alone and had anyway described him well. He was quite short for a policeman, but chunky, not running to fat. The pallor of his face matched the colour of his hair: grey turning to white and not a lot of it. A thick dark overcoat reached his knees, and he walked purposefully, hands thrust deep in pockets, an uncompromising air about him, pugnacious in his urge to get away from there and put some distance between himself and death.

As the man drew level, Blore stepped out into the avenue. "Excuse me. Er – Charles Whitlow?"

The man switched him a tetchy glance, kept walking. "What of it?"

"Um, my name's Jerry Blore. Detective Inspector McCallum said I'd find you here."

Whitlow slowed to a halt, wheezing slightly. He looked at Blore with hard eyes and a cynical grin.

"You don't say. Wonder how long it took Thames Valley's own Nancy Drew to work that one out?" He nodded back in the direction of the grave. "If you'd ever told my old guv'nor his successor would be wearing frilly knickers, he'd've – well, I bet he's started revolving already."

"She –er, thought you might be able to help me?"

"How nice of her to think of me. So what's it about, Mr. Bore?"

"Um – Blore."

"Oh. Right. Sorry."

Blore was feeling increasingly out of his depth. Mary McCallum had given him some idea of what to expect, and once again she'd hit the mark. Of course, she'd been palming him off. Ten seconds of her company had told him she was ambitious and hard as nails. She revelled in her work load, and it had been good of her to spare him five minutes. He knew that because she'd told him so. Minutes in which she made it plain that it had all happened long before her time and she wasn't prepared to give it any consideration now.

In spite of everything, he pressed on. "She told me you worked on the Boyd Neelan case some years back?"

Whitlow pulled a face and shrugged dismissively. "*Some years?* That's an understatement. Try donkey's years, chum. But yes, she's got that one right. And we got

3

it done and dusted inside a couple of days. Straightforward as you could get. So what of it?"

"I don't believe Anita Mead killed him."

The words hung, reedy and tenuous, on the chill air. Blore had wanted to pack some belief into them but, cowed by the other man's effortless antagonism, he'd uttered them without conviction.

Whitlow's laugh was harsh and grating. "You don't believe -? Oh, come *on*. First you shove Madam McCallum in my face, then follow up with this. What is it with you, chum? 'Cos if you're just here to take the piss you showed up on the wrong day. Here's a polite suggestion: why don't you just get on your bike and pedal back to where you came from?"

He turned and stomped off, his footsteps echoing brutally on the hard ground.

"Mr. Whitlow – *please*."

The other man stopped, turned round. Whether at the note of despair in his voice, whether at the sorry, down-at-heel sight of him, Blore didn't know. But Whitlow was quick to cancel out any whiff of compassion: he was exasperated and made no attempt to conceal it.

"Listen, chum. I've just buried an old colleague. His name was Tom Arnison – ex-Detective Chief Superintendent Arnison: a fine man, policeman and guv'nor. I'm off to his wake right now, 'cos he deserves a decent send-off. On the way back to my bus stop there's the Cardigan Arms, on the corner of Brackley Street. I'll meet you there about nine, unless I'm so battered that I forget. If so, tough. And I'm not promising anything, okay? 'Cept that I'll listen to what you've got to say, 'cos that's the way I am. Right?"

He didn't wait for a reply, turning and walking away with more purpose than before. Blore watched him go, grateful for the opportunity to put his point of view, but wondering quite what he was going to say.

And knowing before he began exactly what he was going to hear.

★★★

Blore got to the Cardigan Arms just on nine. He would have settled for anywhere other than a pub, but was pretty sure from that first brief acquaintance that Whitlow wouldn't have been open to negotiation.

He doubted that the man would show up anyway, in which case he'd have reached a dead end before he'd begun. McCallum's pushing him on to Arnison's former sidekick had been all he was likely to get out of her.

Blore had believed he was ready to handle being inside a pub again. But the moment he pushed through the swing door he was fazed by the fog of smoke, the gabble of voices, shrieks of laughter; by the merry clink of glasses and press of people round the bar.

And then the sixties' music: funny how even now, almost thirty years on, it was always sixties' music. Surely it was time to move on: flog some other unsuspecting decade to death. Blore almost chuckled. *Move on?* Fine example he was setting.

He stood dithering. He felt marooned, because everything was going on around him, and these days he felt hemmed in, whereas before he'd been right there in the middle of it, a partaker at the feast. Places like this with their relentless thumping background beat and atmosphere of booze-swilling vibrancy had been home from home. Night after night straight from work to a pub, sometimes for a short burst, other times, particularly after a trying day, for a longer session. Until every day had become a trying day.

Blore felt the growing urge to turn and bolt, knowing that to do so would be to reduce his purpose, his sole *raison-d'etre* to a joke; much like the rest of his life. He was saved by the swish of the door opening behind him, a heavy hand clamping down on his shoulder.

"Wotcher, chum. What's your poison?"

He turned to encounter Whitlow, standing not quite steadily, a crooked grin and some colour bequeathed by several drinks alleviating his pallor.

"Mr. Whitlow. Please – I'll get them."

"My shout, lad. What'll it be?"

"Er, just Perrier water, please."

The man was scrutinising him carefully, peering as if he couldn't see him clearly, and Blore braced himself for a snide remark along the lines of *"Can't face up to a man's drink, then?"* Some put-down like that.

But to his surprise the grin widened; not, he thought, unkindly. "You on the wagon?"

"Permanently." *My name is Jeremy Blore: I am an alcoholic.*

"Fair play. Why don't you take a seat?" Whitlow indicated a vacant corner table and Blore, nodding his thanks, made his way over there.

Whitlow was back inside a couple of minutes, time Blore had spent dumbly studying the stains and scratches on the table, and set down a glass of Perrier decorated with a dainty slice of lemon in front of him. His own foaming pint followed with a thud, beer vaulting the rim of the glass and forming a pool on the table. Whitlow scraped back his chair and collapsed into it, took a large slurp and sighed. "Ah, that's more like it. Beats the piss I've just been drinking hands down."

Blore primly sipped his mineral water. "It went well? The wake?"

Whitlow shrugged. He'd lost the grin and looked morose again. "Well enough." He drank again, deeply, then set down his glass and stared thoughtfully at Blore.

Blore wondered what he saw. A pale, emaciated man in his late forties dressed in an ill-fitting suit? It didn't tell the whole story, but he guessed that Whitlow understood. The suffering was plain to see, echoing through the obvious nervousness, the shake of the hand which held the glass, the tentative speech and whole edge-of-seat aura about him. Blore didn't want questions, certainly not about himself. He was here for answers.

Neither did he like the silence. "Mr. Whitlow, I –"

"It's Chas." Whitlow remained unsmiling. "We needn't be formal."

"Jerry."

The other man nodded distractedly, twirled his glass round a couple of times. "Okay. Now, before we go any further. This business of Neelan's murder. I told you before, and I'll say it again: it was done and dusted at the time. In fact, me and Tom Arnison knocked it on the head in two days flat. So you can trawl away on the Internet to your heart's content, study every word of ever Neelan biography ever spawned. Everything'll reach the same conclusion: *she did it.* Then ran away and topped herself out of remorse. It was a crime of passion, chum. As old as sin."

Blore caught the note of resignation and felt annoyed by it. "But will you listen for a moment – *please?*"

"Sure I'll listen," Whitlow replied equably. "I said I would. But first things first. I could use another drink."

"Here, let me." Blore delved in a pocket and hauled out a crumpled five-pound note.

"Cheers." As he'd hoped, Whitlow leaned across and prised it from his grasp. "I'll get 'em, shall I? What's yours?"

"Oh – no, not for me, thanks."

The other man nodded, and Blore knew he'd seen the haunting. He'd not gone up to a bar himself since those dark days immediately after Cassie, when it had finally dawned upon him after that last mammoth binge that he needed help. He was grateful that Whitlow had sussed that.

But he was again ill-at-ease under the scrutiny; it felt as if Whitlow was staring into the depths of his being. Blore knew what was there and wasn't proud of it.

"A-Anita Mead," he gabbled. "I knew her well, you see."

"Sure, chum. But all this happened – when? – close on thirty years ago. Why now? She's long gone. Some of the others too. Who d'you suppose this is going to help?"

He had no answer except to nod grudgingly and lower his gaze. Whitlow was frowning, but even so Blore sensed his sympathy. Without another word, the ex-detective sergeant rose and went over to the bar.

Blore watched him go, feeling inadequacy and hesitation wash over him. How could he explain? How could he say *I found her photograph the other day*? How explain that he'd only just come back to life with a jolt, after long years in a steadily descending hell got the monkey off his back to be – at last – clean again and somewhere approaching wholesome?

And now, only now, going through Mum's things, discarding some, keeping others, spiriting her clothes away to a charity shop – *only now*, when Annie's photo had slithered out between the pages of a book, Annie grinning cheekily, at once coy and brassy, ditzy and amusing. He'd simply stared at it and remembered: she's been gone *years*. But even so the sadness had flooded back in one big sucker punch, and all the hurting, hurting he'd blocked out for all those years, its pain cushioned first, deliciously, by Cassie, then inevitably by the bottle.

Whitlow returned, setting down his glass with a quiet *thunk*, coaxing him out of his reverie, steering him back to the matter in hand.

He looked up. "It's a long story, Mr. Whitlow. I won't waste your time with it all. But, well, I've been *away,* and here I am, back at last. Annie and I, we were, well, boy- and girlfriend, long before she met Boyd Neelan. And I feel I owe her this, you see. To her memory. I knew her well, and she was no killer."

"Seems to me you're saying you loved her, chum."

He glanced up sharply, expecting to encounter a sneering cynicism. But Whitlow's face was serious, and Blore's surprise must have shown.

"Yes," he burbled. "Yes, I suppose I am." *Love before he'd known love's meaning; and even once he'd known it, he'd been just as adept at throwing it away.*

"Jerry, honey, I'm splitting. I reckon it's now or never, so I'm off to the big, bad city. Fancy coming along? We could shack up together, see how it works out?"

"Come off it, Annie. Not another shopping trip? 'Sides, I'm not off again until Thursday."

Shops were like a drug to Anita. Carnaby Street, Biba, boutique after boutique. He'd tag along dutifully, bored after the first hour, while she could go on long enough to make them nearly miss their train. The shop where she worked didn't pay well, and he guessed she must spend every last penny on clothes and shoes. And then she'd start to badger him, promise him paradise that night, and he'd make her yet one more loan which he knew he'd never see again.

"No, sweetie, I'm off for keeps. This town's the pits, and I'm going nowhere fast. Anyway, I've had it up to here with Mr. Podgy Presswick and his square old shop, and him squeezing my bum every time he reckons no-one's looking. *(With Annie in those microscopic skirts, there was a case to be made for him succumbing to temptation).* And you know how it is with my mum – blasted out of her skull most of the time. Oh Jerry, babe, this is something I've just got to do: get me a job in some fancy pub or club, dance the night away – every night. And you and me, well, like we could find some groovy little pad and shack up, and p'raps you could work in one of them big Oxford Street stores. How about it, baby? What d'you say?"

He knew it'd kill his mum long before her time, even if this was 1969 and peace and love were high on everyone's agenda. But he didn't say that, quickly weighing up his options instead. She'd been his first girl, and even now he didn't know what she'd seen in him, didn't think she could be serious about him because she seldom was about anything else. Couldn't believe it was him she wanted for all the times they'd made love, those wicked, giggling, stolen hours of sheer abandonment. He was slow, a bit strait-laced (thanks, Mum), dependable, wanting to carve a career out of a poor upbringing. They seemed like chalk and cheese. But perhaps that was the answer: that he offered her a security and certainty she'd never had, something new and startling in her dishevelled life.

11

Patiently he pointed out that old Fender was due to retire in a couple of months, and that his boss had let it be known that he'd consider him for the position. Departmental manager at nineteen and a pay rise, a big one, guaranteed. Despite all the loans he'd made Anita, he'd almost saved enough for the deposit on a flat.

She laughed at the suggestion. "Jerry, you're such an old stick-in-the-mud. Can you see me slaving over a kitchen sink? What a gas! Sweetie, life's for *living*. And it's too short anyway, and I just wanna be where it's at, like right now. I may never get another chance." *She wouldn't.*

They'd parted soon after, parted best of friends with all the usual promises to keep in touch. For a while, he'd been torn in two. Sad to see her go, but a parting of the ways had always been the inevitable ending. They'd come from poor backgrounds, both fatherless, and they each had ambitions, but in a different key, charming them to different destinations. He supposed it was just as well, because there was no way he might have expected her to be the docile, stay-at-home little wife. For there was in Annie that ludicrous devil-may-care streak which excited and frightened him off in equal measure.

His mum had been more forthright. "I've always said that Mead girl's no better than she should be. Can't think what you saw in her, Jeremy. But thank the Lord she's cleared off. *London,* indeed! Perhaps now you'll find yourself a decent girl."

Not for years, Mum. Not until Cassie. And then I chased her away.

Blore pushed the years aside, alert to Whitlow studying him over the rim of his glass. He guessed what was coming; guessed wrongly. He hadn't expected compassion to be on Whitlow's agenda.

"You're saying she was no killer, and you're entitled to your opinion. I'm willing to help where I can – beats sitting in an armchair staring at the fireplace. But only so's you can find out for yourself. Facts don't lie, see, Jerry. The case is long closed. I can give you a start, point you at the people who were around then. Speak to them if they'll let you, 'cos they're not obliged to give you the time of day. After that you'll have to join up the dots by yourself. That's if there are any dots to join."

2

Whitlow was already well-fuelled, but that didn't stop him taking on a couple more pints during his narrative. And he went on to give Blore chapter and verse, whether he wanted it or not.

Boyd Neelan had come over from County Cork early in 1965, penniless and determined to make his way on to the pop music scene. Blore had seen early footage of him, amateur stuff, gawky and self-conscious with the Beatle cut they'd all reckoned was their passport to fame, plus dark suit, narrow tie, drainpipe trousers and chisel-toed, elastic-sided boots.

It had been Ned Hargreaves who'd 'discovered' him, singing in a Sunday night slot in a barn behind a down-at-heel pub in Haringey. He was fronting a group destined for nowhere: Timmy and the Tomahawks. But in spite of the less than salubrious backdrop, he seemed to have something which picked him out from the crowd.

Hargreaves was a journalist with ideas way above his station. He wanted to write about pop, but *Melody Maker* and *New Musical Express* wouldn't touch him, so he worked for a short-lived rag called *Thames Courier*, covering magistrates' courts, local squabbles and, when the editor wasn't feeling strong enough to resist him, the occasional record review. Ned had two things going for him: he didn't mind making a nuisance of himself and wouldn't take 'no' for an answer. He smartened up Boyd and put him in the way of the right people; ditched the Tomahawks and promoted him as a solo artist under his own name.

It wasn't enough. Boyd cut a couple of demos but still sounded raw. There were no takers.

But it would have taken more than that to discourage Ned Hargreaves. He wormed his way into Nicky Royce's good graces and talked him into trying out Boyd. That was another of Ned's gifts: vision.

Royce was in his mid-twenties then, a budding singer-songwriter. The songs were okay: punchy lyrics and the kind of beat that British Pop was all about. It was just that Royce's own voice was a little too thin to do them justice. He'd formed his own group the year before, the Makeweights, along with his long-time pal Phil Duggan, one of the best drummers around. They'd flirted with the bottom end of the charts a couple of times, and Ned was convinced they had it in them to go higher.

So he suggested what Nicky knew in his heart was the way to go: the Makeweights needed a front man. Duggan had the drums, Royce penned the potential hits and played a mean lead guitar, so the next step wasn't rocket science.

Because Boyd had the looks, the voice and before long the swagger and confidence to deliver the goods.

So with Hargreaves ducking and diving as their manager (Ned was good at that too), things started to happen. *Ready, Steady, Go, Top of the Pops,* and *Sunday Night at the London Palladium* all came along in turn, and a serious assault on the charts began. Suddenly the Beatles, Stones and Hollies weren't having it all their own way.

All eyes focused on the front man. Royce and Duggan, indisputably the group's engine room, tended to leave things in Boyd's increasingly extrovert hands. More vision from Ned, and they turned into Boyd Neelan and the Makeweights; and the hits kept coming.

Then, about eighteen months on, at the height of the 1967 Summer of Love, Boyd found himself dead centre of the public gaze, thanks to his romance with Suzy Steller.

Suzy wasn't far behind Twiggy and Jean Shrimpton. She started off as a model but soon sidetracked into acting via TV game shows and soppy sitcoms. She quickly graduated to bit parts then bigger parts in films, mainly near-the-knuckle comedies. With the looks and curves mandatory to success, practically all her appearances saw her wearing as little as possible.

Suzy and Boyd were linked by a common bond: they were voraciously ambitious and quickly saw how each could enhance the other's career. They met, smooched and hopped into bed at a high-profile Soho party. The teen mags were full of them and launched them on a whirlwind courtship. Ned Hargreaves was never far away to ensure maximum publicity. ("The little weasel never missed a trick," Whitlow growled). Neelan-Steller was one of 1968's top celebrity weddings, and the media gorged themselves on the prospect. The TV mags and lurid Sundays overflowed with pull-out supplements, posing such inane questions as *What Will Suzy Wear On Their Wedding Night?*'

Suzy had a big effect on Boyd's career: for a while the media pursued them everywhere, and even the Beatles' relationships were put in the shade. But what Boyd hadn't foreseen was how much of a lift he'd given Suzy. The clothing issue aside, she had some ability as an actress, and a few plum roles happened her way.

Thus their careers began to bear them in different directions. Not that Suzy would ever be content to be the little wife, but it helped ensure that the parting of the ways came early. In late 1969, Suzy even cut a disc with a session group, the Suzettes. It was utter tripe, and as such became the Christmas Number One, bringing Suzy and her cheesily grinning group an appearance on every seasonal show imaginable. Boyd was seriously, but seriously, miffed.

They started to fall out, and naturally the worst quarrels erupted in the most public places, almost as if Ned Hargreaves had planned it that way. They were seen in the company of other people, and the papers had a field day. Each seemed to be trying to outdo the other, and if that wasn't enough their work was forcing them further and further apart.

By now Boyd had attained pin-up status, and empty-headed girls were queuing up to get laid. He was in seventh heaven, developing a real hunger for women; with a 'love 'em and leave 'em' philosophy which ensured that no-one hung around too long.

"Your girlfriend was the latest in a long line." Whitlow wasn't pulling punches, and Blore found to his surprise that he respected that. "Silly tarts were starry-eyed, believing his easy assurances that he was going to turn them into stars. Nearest they got was staring up at 'em in the night sky."

After his death Boyd attained super-stardom, and Suzy didn't come out of it badly either. Amid all the razzmatazz surrounding their wedding, they'd seen fit to make wills in one another's favour. 'Till death us do part' and all that. Prophetic.

So Suzy ended up with the entire package: house with several acres in Oxfordshire, swish pad in Belgravia, villa in Spain. Then there were royalties from 'Greatest Hits' albums, churned out every couple of years by the marketing luminaries, as well as documentaries, biographies, a tribute group. Suzy couldn't lose.

Perhaps the only thing that hurt was that Boyd turned into something of a legend, acquiring the charisma which emanated from stars who'd died young. He'd be mentioned in the same breath as Hendrix and Joplin, who'd passed on the year before him.

Steller had the best motive for wanting him dead, but why should she need it? They were practically living apart, she had no shortage of rich lovers and was wealthy in her own right. In later life she took to the stage. Her body wasn't as marketable as it once had been, but she compensated by pulling out the stops on the acting front. She was in great demand, busier than ever before; indeed too much so to be bothered to play the grieving widow.

★★★

They'd called the house 'Dreamfields': Suzy's choice. It lay just outside the sleepy South Oxfordshire village of Chelfold, a tribute to Edwardian architecture, red-brick with bulging casements, patterned timber gables and french windows opening out on to flower-strewn balconies. The grounds rolled on forever, making employment for three gardeners, while off to the side of the house Boyd had a separate annexe built, fairly tasteless, which he used as a studio, general bolt-hole and a place to take his women.

After the first flush of wedded bliss had passed, Suzy spent little time at Dreamfields. Most of her work was in London at various theatres and film studios, so she used the Belgravia flat as a base.

Nicky Royce and his wife Stephanie lived farther down the road in Chelfold itself, and a lot more modestly. Stephanie got embroiled in numerous village activities, and Nicky often tagged tamely along, with the result that the villagers quickly warmed to them. The Royces raised a great deal of money for various causes, as well as hosting an annual fireworks party in their grounds.

Nicky and Boyd used the Dreamfields studio for their work, collaborating closely on song-writing and recording.   Royce/Neelan   weren't   quite Lennon/McCartney. Most of the work was Nicky's anyway, although Boyd contributed here and there with the lyrics. *'Need Ya, Baby'* was the most lucrative of his efforts. Pretty basic, lacking Royce's finesse, it wouldn't have charted anywhere near as well if Boyd hadn't been at the height of his fame when they'd recorded it.

The village didn't see a lot of Boyd – although one or two village girls did. They were put off by the imposing wrought-iron gates, imposing even when they were flung wide open; put off by the sports cars screeching through the village bearing their burdens to Boyd's all-night parties, which were role models in excess: the champagne flowing, music blaring, voices shrill, ecstatic, bedrooms full to bursting and naked, boozed-up bodies cavorting after midnight in the swimming pool.

Nicky Royce didn't share Boyd's lifestyle. He was in love with his wife. Stephanie was attractive, strong-willed and feisty, keeping him so well in check that the thought of straying probably never entered his head. Although to be fair, he just wasn't that sort of guy. The Royces would appear at Dreamfields parties but never stayed long: it simply wasn't their scene. That sort of behaviour was beneath them, and besides, Stephanie was ambitious for her husband. She'd recognised his talent the first day she'd set eyes on him, expected him to go places and wasn't keen on Boyd stealing what she saw as his thunder.

Phil Duggan remained even further aloof, never having conformed to the public image of drugged-up, bed-hopping pop star. A gentle and thoughtful man, he'd married Ginny, his childhood sweetheart. They had a young son, Bobby, and lived at the bottom of a quiet lane in Meredown, a village several miles distant from Chelfold.

The Makeweights set-up suited Duggan. He was very much in Neelan's shadow and to a lesser extent Royce's. It never seemed to bother him. Devoted to his wife and son, he was content to do the job he loved and let others take the accolades if that was what turned them on.

So with a drummer who lived for his family and work and Nicky Royce immersed in his song-writing, guitar-playing and backing vocals, Boyd was free to pursue ambition until he choked on it.

The Neelan-Steller union started to crumble soon after it had begun. Suzy might well have been content to hang on in there if Boyd hadn't been so utterly self-centred. They were the Posh and Becks of the late 1960s, a bonus to one another's careers, although Boyd saw himself above Suzy in that respect. He refused to be in thrall to a mere woman and was determined to put her in her place, so he started to play around. Before long, Suzy showed that she could match him in that department. Her ego ran Boyd's pretty close, and she refused point-blank to be made to look foolish.

With Suzy more or less a fixture in the Belgravia flat, Boyd had the brainwave that he'd need someone to run Dreamfields, apart from the cook, cleaner, gardeners and handymen. So he employed a housekeeper, then another; and another.

"None of 'em lasted long," Whitlow said. "But he maintained he had to have them, and you can bet your cotton socks he did. Which is where your girlfriend came in. She was a dancer in one of the London clubs Boyd frequented. They met, clicked and bingo! she was suddenly a housekeeper. She'd been in place a couple of months at the time of his death. She must have had something – her predecessors never lasted half as long."

★★★

Boyd Neelan was at home on the morning he died. He'd been at the piano in the annexe since before nine, thrashing out a new song. This was *'Nowhere To Go'*, which Nicky Royce finished off. It was to give the Makeweights a monster hit, which they dedicated to Boyd's memory.

Blore recalled it storming the charts in the weeks after Boyd's death. It was classic Makeweights material: the unforgiving thump of Duggan's drums, Royce's quirky guitar riffs. But without Neelan's supercharged voice, his innuendoes, Neelan strutting his stuff, lording it over the audience in his dazzling sequinned outfits. Instead it was Nicky's voice, powered by emotion, each word a testament to his dead friend, unashamed tears blotching his face.

> *What can I do, what can I say?*
> *Nowhere to go, and all of today,*
> *I've sat and cried,*
> *And now my tears have dried,*
> *You're still so gone, so far away…*

Anita Mead joined Boyd around ten. He'd asked for an early lunch, something simple which she could stick in the oven before making herself scarce. He was expecting a visitor for an important discussion and didn't want anyone else around.

Nicky Royce dropped by. Anita met him at the door and warned him that Boyd was in a bit of a strop. It was clear the song wasn't going well: Neelan had painted himself into a corner with it – '*Nowhere To Go*' fast going nowhere. Nicky hung around long enough to make a few suggestions, beefing up the lyrics.

He soon called it a day though, because Boyd wasn't in the mood. Annie had told him a visitor was imminent, but she had no idea who it was. Royce could see Boyd was tense and stuck around a while in case he wanted to confide in him. But he soon saw there was little point, said goodbye and left.

Anita accompanied him outside, remarking that Boyd was like a bear with a sore head, and she needed a break. Royce was about to get into his car, when a yellow MG careered into the drive in a wide, screeching arc and skidded to a halt a few yards past him, squirting gravel everywhere. Suzy Steller was at the wheel and leapt out almost before the car had stopped. She looked livid and, on spotting Anita lighting a cigarette in the doorway, let fly with a volley of abuse. Anita looked terrified and made a hurried exit into the shrubbery. Suzy didn't pursue her. Instead she stomped into the annexe and slammed the door with such force that the glass rattled. Nicky heard angry raised voices: Boyd's, with Suzy's shrilling banshee-like above it. Their language was an education, and Royce, not wishing to referee, got in the car and made for home.

According to Steller, she and Boyd continued to argue: the usual thing about infidelities on both sides, with neither of them giving an inch. Once she'd yelled herself to a standstill, Suzy stormed out, slamming the door again. She swung the car round and almost succeeded in clobbering Anita as she scurried out of the shrubbery, causing her to dodge smartly back to safety. Suzy later recalled that, as she bombed off down the drive, she noticed in her mirror that Anita had once more emerged from hiding and was making her way cautiously back to the annexe.

The caller Boyd had been expecting was Phil Duggan. They'd been due to talk about Phil's future with the group. Boyd was concerned about Phil's image – or lack of it – and behind everyone's back had taken it upon himself to sound out a replacement.

Nicky Royce had guessed something like this was in the wind. Boyd hadn't consulted him, because he knew Nicky simply wouldn't hear of it. But Boyd was the main man, getting to the stage where he reckoned his word should be law and throwing his toys out of the pram whenever anyone stood up to him.

Phil Duggan had arranged to be there at eleven and was, as always, punctual, arriving a few minutes after Suzy had left. As he drew up, Anita Mead dashed out of the annexe. She was staggering along, sobbing bitterly. Duggan got out of the car and called to her, but she turned her face away and hurried past him. It was only then he noticed she was carrying a carving-knife, its blade and her hands smeared with blood. As she quickened her pace to hurry away from him, the knife fell to the ground.

Duggan had his young son Bobby with him. The boy had got out of the car and was staring bemusedly after Anita. Phil picked him up, deposited him back in his seat and locked him in. He made after Anita, but she'd reached Boyd's white Mustang, which was parked up by the house. She jumped in, started up and ploughed off down the drive, causing Duggan to leap aside. He could only stare helplessly after her as she turned out on to the road and sped away.

Aware of Bobby distressed and tearful in the car, Duggan made his way to the annexe, filled with apprehension. He found Boyd on the floor in a pool of blood; felt for a pulse and found none. His senses began to fade, and he remembered Bobby, knew he had to be strong for him. Before returning to reassure him, Phil dialled 999 from the phone in the annexe.

★★★

The police didn't find the Mustang until early the following morning. It had been left in the car park at Didcot station. There was a travel rug, smeared with blood, which had been flung on to the back seat. It turned out that the blood was Neelan's.

They made inquiries at the station. It had been a busy Saturday, and the various clerks and station staff had only vague memories of her. No-one could be sure whether she'd boarded a train for London, Oxford or the coast. Appeals were launched on TV and radio for anyone who might have information to come forward. It was likely to be some time before they got results.

As things turned out, Anita had headed for the coast and the resort of Mardon Regis. She booked into a guest house, a bungalow near the sea front called 'Seabirds' and signed her name as 'Susan Starr'. The landlady, a garrulous, kindly soul named Ethel Robey, immediately felt something wasn't right. The girl was clearly ill-at-ease, and Mrs Robey guessed she was on the run from somewhere or someone.

It was late September, nearing the end of the season, and the guest house was practically deserted. The next morning, after breakfast, Anita came to Mrs Robey in a state of great agitation. There was a parade of shops opposite and Anita, about to return to her room, had seen someone she recognised. "I think he might call here. If he does, *please* say I've gone." She pointed out the man, but he was too far away for Ethel Robey to see clearly, and afterwards she was only able to provide a vague description of him.

Anita went to her room. The next time Mrs Robey saw her was on a mortuary slab. Fifteen minutes later, she went along to the girl's room to ask if she wanted her to call the police, but Anita had done a bunk. When Ethel looked out of the lounge window, the man, too, had gone.

She busied herself with serving the other guests. Once they'd left and she was clearing things away, she happened to switch on a portable TV she kept in the kitchen and heard a news bulletin about a search for a girl in connection with the death of Boyd Neelan. *"She may have headed for London or the Mardon Regis area…"* Mrs Robey needed no further prompting. She telephoned the police.

Having questioned her, they searched the town, paying particular attention to the bus and train stations. Towards the end of the day a report came in about the discovery of a body in the Mar estuary a few miles inland. Ethel Robey identified Anita, and this was later confirmed by the Royces and Phil Duggan. Further investigation concluded that she must have jumped from a bridge a few hundred yards upstream from where she was found. The coroner's verdict was that, overcome by what she'd done, she'd taken her own life.

"So as I said before," Whitlow concluded, setting down his empty glass and waving away the offer of a refill, "it was done and dusted at the time. Cut and dried, dead and buried. There's nothing to investigate, my friend."

Blore snatched at the only available straw. "But there's a gap, isn't there? The man at Mardon Regis, watching the guest house from the parade of shops. Who was he?"

Whitlow gave a tired smile: he'd seen this coming. "No-one knows. Ethel's description was a loose one: the man was some distance away, and she couldn't distinguish his features. Neither did Anita mention a name. We made some inquiries and got zip. We wondered if it had been a ruse she'd cooked up. Having realised Ethel was suspicious, she got her to focus on some innocent bystander while she slipped quietly away.

"And in any case." Whitlow's tone had hardened, blunt with a challenge. "The man we buried today was the officer in charge. He was a good copper who swept in all the corners. If there'd been any doubt, any at all, he'd have acted upon it."

Blore could see he wasn't going to get any more. He thanked Whitlow in a voice which couldn't mask his despondency, scraped back his chair and stood up. He offered his hand, and Whitlow shook it, not bothering to get up. After the amount he'd put away in the last few hours, Blore had to wonder if that might prove difficult. He left his mobile number but guessed the ex-DS would probably succeed in losing it. He made his way back to where he'd left his car.

He cast his mind back to the day when news of the tragedy had reached the ears of his local community.

"To think – she served me any number of times in Presswick's – always seemed to be staring into space – drugs, I dare say. But who'd have *thought* it, a local girl and all? Mind you, that mother of hers never brought her up proper. Why, she'd be roaming the streets at night even when she was a tiny slip of a thing. And as to the father – well, it could have been anyone. No, I don't like to speak ill of the dead, but that Mead girl was a real bad lot."

Blore recalled the opening shots from a TV series of the time, *Mission Impossible*. Something about 'disavowing all knowledge'. That's what the whole community had done where Annie was concerned. Her mother, a sad alcoholic, soon moved away. Probably drank herself to death, but who was he to throw stones? He remembered his mum being particularly scathing, very much 'I told you so'.

And he, in the end, was no better than the rest. A promotion came up: assistant store manager in Birmingham. He leapt at the chance: moved away, stayed away, met new friends and pushed Annie so far to the back of his mind she dropped off the shelf. He never mentioned her because he never remembered her, soon to start on his own rollercoaster journey to hell and back.

Yes, Chas, perhaps you were right: I'm on a guilt trip. Should I have gone with her to London? Would I have been strong enough to make such a difference in her life that she'd be alive today? And right again – I'm wasting my time. I can't make a difference to her now, because she's long past caring. Perhaps what I'm trying to do is to show she mattered – even though the time's long gone.

3

Blore couldn't believe his ears when his phone rang late that evening, and the caller turned out to be Whitlow.

"I take it you're determined to push on with this?" No name, no introductory small talk. The ex-DS wasn't one for hanging around.

Blore struggled to answer. He'd been about to turn in, feeling low, wondering what, if anything, he was going to do about tomorrow. At another time, if there'd been a bottle in the house... He pushed the thought away. If he'd achieved nothing else, he'd put *that* behind him.

"Er, well, yes. It's something I've got to do. Perhaps what you said was right: that it's a guilt trip. Even so - ."

He was burbling, and Whitlow cut in decisively. "Right. Okay. Listen, I can give you some details, addresses and the like. 'Cos one thing's for sure, Jerry old son, you won't get another peep out of Inspector

Fancypants with her oh-so-busy flipping schedule. And I've got a point to prove. The juices are still flowing, y'know, and I'm not ready to be put out to grass yet. 'Sides, with me along, it might just persuade Royce, Steller and Ginny Duggan at least to give you a hearing."

Blore wondered how much Whitlow had drunk. He'd been well on the way when he'd left him at the pub and was probably now nipping at the scotch, spurred on by injured pride and the frustration at having been sidelined. A nightcap, then another and so on. Blore knew the road only too well.

Even so, he couldn't believe what he was hearing. But he thanked Whitlow all the same, knowing it'd be a bonus to have him along; and an unlooked-for one at that.

There was no stopping the ex-DS. "No sweat. We'll start with Nicky Royce. Pretty sure he'll give us a hearing. Perhaps you'd phone ahead in the morning, Jerry, and then get back to me. It'll sound better coming from you."

Blore took down Royce's number, then, thoroughly bushed, went to bed and slept, for him, reasonably well. The qualms set in as he awoke, and he wondered if he was about to make a fool of himself. It had all happened nearly *thirty* years ago. But he'd psyched himself up to come this far and knew he had to see it through to whatever the conclusion might be.

He phoned Royce and, after some bumbling around, explained who he was and what he wanted. Royce didn't say a lot, patiently hearing him out. "Okay," he cut in at last. "That's cool, long as you're on the level. It turns out that you're some sort of journo, and I'll pull the plug on it, right? My privacy means a lot to me. But I don't mind talking about the past. Sometimes it seems that's all that's left."

Blore mentioned that a former policeman would be accompanying him. Just a guiding hand, really. He took pains to emphasise that this was in no way official: DI McCallum had made it clear she wasn't interested in reopening the case.

Royce told him it was cool again, they arranged the time and ended the call pleasantly enough. He phoned Chas and agreed to pick him up within the hour. Whitlow lived at Kidlington, some fifteen miles away.

They had to pass Dreamfields to get to Royce's house in Chelfold village. It was now an expensive nursing home. Whitlow got him to pull in to the side of the road and pointed out where the annexe had been. It had been replaced by a palatial wing tacked on to the already large house. The lawns had a manicured look, and the gleaming wrought-iron gates bore a name which wasn't Dreamfields. Blore recalled the line of a hymn from his schooldays: *They fly forgotten as a dream.* He supposed Boyd wasn't forgotten: he lived on in his music, yet one more icon of the swinging sixties. The same couldn't be said for Anita, but they were both equally dead.

As they drove on down the road, Whitlow explained that the Royces still lived in the house Nicky and Stephanie had bought in the mid-1960s. He'd remarried five or six years after her death, his second wife nearly thirty years his junior.

The house was called 'Songrise', a much simpler affair than Dreamfields and a lot more modern, stone-built with a double garage to the side, in front of whose doors stood a silver BMW and a cornflower-blue Peugeot 206. A semi-circle of garden, bright with rudbeckia and climbing roses, fanned round between the entrance and exit gates.

The bell-pull set off a melodious chime deep in the house. Blore recognised the opening bars of *'Believe In Tomorrow'*, the words springing at him from out of the years:

> *I'll say goodbye to sorrow.*
> *It's your sweet love*
> *That keeps me sane,*
> *Helps me believe in tomorrow…*

After a short pause the door was opened by a tall blonde woman in her mid-thirties. She was dressed stylishly in a frilly cream blouse, mottled grey-white skirt and low-heeled court shoes and was attractive despite the severity of her expression.

"Yes?"

Two of them standing there po-faced: she probably had them down for Jehovah's Witnesses.

Haltingly, Blore explained who they were, and that they'd called to talk to Nicky Royce about Boyd Neelan. He was expecting them.

Her mouth tightened some more. Blore felt she was too polite to slam the door in their faces, but only because they'd been invited. Left to her, it might have been a close-run thing.

"I hope this isn't for some magazine," she said tartly.

Blore tried to placate her with a smile. "I've assured Mr Royce that it's nothing to do – "

"Or some potential biography. There seems to be one every few months. After all this time, I should have thought every angle had been exhausted."

"This is different," Blore burbled uneasily. "I – I was a friend of Anita Mead."

"Who? Oh – I see. The girl who -."

Blore didn't want to have to justify himself to Lorraine Royce. It wasn't her he'd come to see. And he didn't think she'd have much sympathy with his tenuous motive: *something I have to do.*

But at that moment a light footfall sounded behind her. She half-turned as her husband joined her, one hand at her shoulder, the other at her waist, easing her ever so gently aside.

Blore had seen many photographs of Nicky Royce, both from the distant and recent past. Some from his heyday in the late sixties and early seventies; a few from seven or eight years back, when he still performed the occasional gig.

Never a tall man, he'd become slightly stooped. His face was a little puffy, hair receding, almost completely grey and tied back in a pony tail. He'd always been thin, was even thinner now, and Blore immediately suspected that he might be ill. His eyes, calm and grey, were watchful. He wore faded blue jeans, a white shirt with the cuffs popped back and brown moccasins. His manner, no surprise from all Blore had heard and read, was studied and courteous.

"Jerry Blore? Thanks for phoning ahead. Appreciate it." He stuck out a hand, and they shook. His eyes were already appraising Whitlow. A spasm of – what? – surprise, shock even, flashed across his face.

"I should know your name. Good Lord, you – weren't you -?"

"On the original inquiry," Whitlow cut in equably. "You've a good memory, Mr Royce. Detective Sergeant Charles Whitlow, retired now. I'm just here to keep Mr Blore company, and he's here – well, I suppose to have his mind set at rest. There's nothing official about this. Quite honestly, you're not obliged to give us the time of day."

Royce grinned back, a trifle uncertainly in Blore's opinion, and flicked a glance at his wife. "Oh, we're not like that, are we, Lori? Perhaps you'd make us some coffee, while I take these gents through to the lounge."

He patted her companionably on the shoulder, was rewarded with a brief half-smile, and then she turned without a word and headed down the hallway, presumably to the kitchen. Aware that the ensuing pause could turn unpleasant, Royce busily ushered his visitors inside and through to a large room.

He'd called it a lounge, but to Blore there was nothing comfortable about it. A chandelier hung dead centre of the ceiling, the wallpaper was ornate and heavy, the furniture probably antique: an oak sideboard, two chesterfields, a *chaise-longue* and a sprawling walnut coffee table, its surface polished to a mirror-like sheen. The house itself was relatively modern, the room elderly through its possessions. Blore felt its atmosphere bordered on cloying.

Incongruously dotted about the walls were various platinum and gold discs, all celebrating Nicky's compositions. *'Long Time Gone', 'Crazy Heart'* and *'Believe In Tomorrow'* had been the big hits, their performances all Boyd-driven, yet dwarfed by *'Nowhere To Go'*, the Makeweights' tribute to their dead lead singer, the song he'd been working on that fateful morning, the song he'd struggled to get right, and which Nicky had had to mould into a cohesive whole.

But none of these was the centre piece, which held sway on the far wall, again dead centre so that anyone entering the room would find their gaze immediately drawn towards it. It was an oil painting, contained in a modest rosewood frame, of a striking woman.

However, Blore was given no time to stare. Royce showed them to seats on one side of the coffee table, while he pitched down opposite them on the *chaise-longue*. He draped his arm round the head-rest and looked his question at Blore.

"I know all the details," Blore said. *Know* was an understatement *par excellence*. He'd read – lived – every Neelan biography in Oxford Central Library, including the supposedly authorised one by Ned Hargreaves; watched footage galore of Neelan with and without the Makeweights; trawled the Internet for newspaper and magazine archives. "All I'm asking is for your version of events on the –um– day it happened."

"It won't change anything." He caught the note of sympathy in Royce's tone.

"Please. All I want are the facts as you witnessed them. Then I can go away and –well– correlate everything I've learned."

"And find a loophole? I doubt if you will, Mr Blore. Anyway, well, that day, the things that happened were earth-shattering. Twenty-eight years ago last month: no way I'll ever forget.

"I left here just before nine-thirty and drove along to Boyd's studio. He'd been trying to get to grips with a song he'd been writing. '*Nowhere To Go*', of course. He'd got into a rut. Boyd would have no trouble starting off a song. It was carrying on where he got into difficulties. He'd had a sizeable hit with '*Need Ya, Baby*', all his own work. But if the lyrics needed something beyond the basic, or the middle eight lacked invention, he'd quickly get hacked off.

"I said I'd run through it with him. He wasn't too chuffed, mainly because he didn't want me claiming co-authorship. It had never sat easy with him that I'd been churning out songs for more than fifteen years, and he was still a bit of a novice. And once he'd started a project, he could be a bit shitty with us all until he'd seen it through.

"As I walked in, he was at the piano. He saw me, crashed both hands down on the keys and let off a torrent of abuse. Anita Mead was there. Boyd was planning a working lunch, and she was supposed to be preparing it. He'd installed a kitchen at the back of the studio – had a bedroom there too, a real home from home. Anyway, Anita was lounging in a chair, having a drag. She greeted me with raised eyebrows and told me she'd make a start preparing his meal. I won't repeat what he said, but he was in a hell of a mood. She scooted off, and he looked up and grinned. "Sorry, Nicko. But you know how it is. Just can't seem to put this baby to bed.""

"I asked him to run through what he had. As I'd guessed, the middle section was a right mess, so I sat down at the piano and went over a couple of ideas. But by then Boyd had lost interest. He went to the window and started messing about with a guitar. He could tag along on rhythm, no sweat, but lead guitarist he wasn't. He flung it down in exasperation and checked his watch.

""Hey, look, sorry, man. I'm expecting somebody along soon, and this ain't panning out. Let's go back to it another time, huh?""

Nicky broke off as the door swung open. They all looked up as Lorraine Royce came in bearing a silver tray with coffee pot, cups and a plate of biscuits. Nicky got to his feet, relieved her of it and set it down on the coffee table.

Lorraine perched on the edge of the *chaise-longue* and asked Blore and Whitlow what they wanted. Her manner was a bit distant but at least polite, as if she'd finally resigned herself to their presence. With refreshments sorted, Royce went on.

"Well, I said goodbye and left, puzzling over who this caller might be. Anita followed me out. She was looking a bit frazzled: she knew Boyd was in a mood and didn't relish being present when he let rip.

"Just then a yellow MG swung off the road and came hammering up the drive. I was about to get in my car, and it missed me by inches. It squealed to a halt, and Suzy Steller got out, without any acknowledgement. Reason was, she'd seen Anita cowering in the doorway and let fly a torrent of invective. Anita, wisely, didn't hit back, just turned and dashed off into the shrubbery. Suzy went inside, and I heard both she and Boyd start ranting. I decided against intervening. I'd got caught in the middle of one of their rows before: trying to mediate was something you didn't do.

"I got in the car and drove home. I'd not long arrived when Suzy shot past in the MG, driving hell for leather. I remember the grandfather clock in the hallway just then striking eleven. That, as I learned afterwards, was the time Phil Duggan and Boyd had arranged to meet. Phil was always punctual – you could set your watch by him. He must have arrived just after Suzy had left.

"It was Phil who found him, and I don't think the poor guy was ever the same afterwards. A gentle soul, old Phil. Lived for his music, his boy and his missis – and I can tell you young Bobby worshipped his dad. Christ knows the agony he went through those last few years of his life, with the cancer raging within him. The memory of what he found couldn't have helped: it stayed with him forever."

By pure chance, Blore happened to look across at Lorraine Royce as Nicky was speaking. She'd been watching her husband, her brow furrowed with concern as he'd talked about Duggan's illness. Blore looked away too late: she caught him observing her, rewarded him with the hint of a smile. He turned his attention back to Nicky, wondering if he too might not be seriously ill.

"Phil put Bobby in the car," Royce was saying, "and ordered him to stay put. He went in and found Boyd sprawled on the floor in a pool of blood, not moving, not responding. He came round to me in a hell of a state – he'd had the presence of mind to phone the police and ambulance from the studio. I sent him back, because he needed to be there to talk to them. I called my neighbour, got her to look after Bobby and went back with Phil. See, I was alone in the house – my wife was shopping up in London. Of course, back in those days there was no way of reaching her, and I remember thinking how much I could have done with her being there. She would have stayed calm, would have taken control."

Blore couldn't avoid switching another glance at Lorraine. This time it was Nicky who noticed it. He laughed. "Oh, I don't mean Lori. She'd have been occupied with her doll's pram somewhere in deepest Hertfordshire. No, Stevie – Stephanie, my first wife. She passed on a few years back."

It was as if someone had pulled a plug, for suddenly all the energy seemed to have drained from Royce, who looked every one of his sixty-two years. His gaze crept up to fasten on the portrait above the fireplace. Blore was conscious of them all following it.

The woman in the portrait stood on a terrace overlooking what Blore guessed was the garden at the back of the house. She wore a long, trailing, burgundy-coloured evening gown, a silver necklace and earrings, and gave the impression of gazing down at the artist with condescension.

She was a striking woman, the high cheekbones, tight smile and fiery gleam in her eyes giving the appearance of haughtiness. Short auburn hair accentuated the sharp outline of her face. Blore reckoned she looked in her early- to mid-forties, and that the portrait had been painted some time after her death.

He recalled that she'd died as the result of an accident, some party on a boat out in the Bay of Biscay. Everyone had been the worse for wear and she'd fallen overboard, her body not recovered until the following day.

He wondered if Nicky was about to elaborate on that as the silence lengthened, but then Whitlow coughed lightly and Blore, realising it was meant for him, tore his gaze from the portrait and got back to the matter in hand.

"So what you're saying, Mr Royce, is that there's no doubt that Anita killed Boyd Neelan? Might it not have been possible that his quarrel with his wife – well, possible that Suzy killed him and Anita came back in, found him and simply picked up the knife, panicked and ran?"

His words hung heavily in the ensuing silence. Whitlow was staring at him intently, maybe trying to convey some message. If so, Blore didn't have a clue what it was. Lorraine was looking at him with disdain, as if he'd said something obscene.

Nicky took his time replying. He seemed to be choosing his words carefully, slowly bringing his gaze round to meet Blore's. He shook his head sadly.

"I'm sorry, Mr Blore. You'll know of the friction between Boyd and Suzy: it was well-documented, the usual problems of a high-profile showbiz marriage. Neither of them was old enough, experienced or selfless enough to cope. I'm not saying Boyd wouldn't have made Anita Mead some sort of promise. He'd offer the earth to his particular fancy of the moment, make her believe she was all that mattered to him. And she'd been at Dreamfields two whole months – a lot longer than any of her predecessors.

"Boyd would have been in a pig of a mood that morning after Suzy had left. They'd been shouting at the tops of their voices, and *she'd* been shouting *him* down. They were going at it hammer and tongs but, believe it or not, Boyd hated such confrontations. I'd known him for – what? - six or seven years by then, and he'd never lost a certain shyness.

"I'd guess that when Anita came back in, she would have said something which pushed him to the edge. He was quick-tempered – that was the Irish in him – and he could be violent when roused. Perhaps he hit her, and she tried to defend herself and ended up knifing him. I doubt for a moment that she intended to kill him. It was a tragedy all round, if only because it was so avoidable. Boyd was a great talent: he could have been so much greater. And Anita had her whole life before her. I'm sorry, Mr Blore, that I'm unable to offer any comfort greater than that."

Blore wasn't satisfied. But he could see that Royce was trying to let him down lightly, and that he was unlikely to get any more from him. He appreciated the sympathy, even though he didn't want it.

Whitlow came in then, and he was grateful for that too. Grateful because he knew he wouldn't have let it go – couldn't – even though he hadn't the faintest idea what his next question would have been.

Chas was asking for Ginny Duggan's address. Phil had been dead three years, a long-running war with bowel cancer, and Whitlow wondered if his widow might have moved. Royce said he had the address somewhere: she and Bobby had taken a smaller cottage in nearby East Stoke. He got up to leave the room, and Whitlow stood too.

"Do you mind if I –uh- use the -?"

"It's this way."

Nicky went, and Chas tagged along. Blore couldn't help wondering if it was a ploy to leave him alone with Lorraine Royce. If so, he wished he hadn't bothered.

He found himself drawn back to the portrait, stood up and shuffled over for a closer look. He pretended to be engrossed in it, giving her an excuse not to have to speak to him.

She declined it, offering him more coffee. Surprised, he accepted. She poured and held out the cup to him.

"So this is a trip down memory lane for you?"

He suspected sarcasm but could discern none in her looks or manner.

"I wouldn't call it that. Anita was -."

"Your girlfriend?"

"Yes. We were both very young. I –um- I mean, it's a long time back in the past and, well, I really ought to have followed it up years ago."

He was bumbling nervously around: typical of him in this new life without booze, without the false, brash confidence it had slyly lent him. She saw it, skipped over it: she was starting to surprise him some more.

"It's a bit of a history lesson for me. Nicky's never really mentioned it. I suppose he reckons it's just that – ancient history, something I never needed to know. After all, I would have been at infants' school about then – with my doll's pram."

Blore noted the bitterness. He didn't know how to respond, but Lorraine saved him the bother by not dwelling on the matter any longer.

"Nicky worked his socks off for that group," she went on. "Neither he nor Phil got the recognition they deserved – they were the engine room, they drove it. But Boyd, as front man, got all the accolades. He revelled in them."

"Might Nicky have resented that?"

She saw what he was getting at, and he prepared himself for a snappish retort. But her reply was considered and equable.

"There's not a jealous bone in his body. He's far too laid-back for his own good. If he's going to get somewhere, it'll be at his pace and in his way: he won't be rushed. I suppose that's partly why he married me: I must be as mild as milk compared to Stevie." She smiled, and her whole demeanour seemed to relax. For a moment, Blore glimpsed behind the mask; long enough to understand that Lorraine Royce was living a role which wasn't the real her.

"Although," she added teasingly, "you might be forgiven for thinking otherwise."

Then her eyes were drawn back to Stephanie's portrait. Stephanie gazing down upon them, as if observing every move with an easy contempt. It seemed as if she might be laughing at them. And the mask was back: Lorraine's eyes were hard and her expression frosty as she jabbed a finger at the portrait.

"She was the driving force. All Nicky ever wanted to do was sit in an attic and write his songs. He wasn't a bad performer: pretty assured on lead guitar, but didn't have what it took vocally. Artistes queued up for his songs – they still do. She propelled him forward, and if he'd gone along with her wishes and taken as much of the limelight as he deserved, Boyd Neelan wouldn't have had a prayer.

"But Boyd was Nicky's excuse, his passport to remaining far enough back in the shadows to satisfy both himself and Stevie. He and Ned Hargreaves discovered

Boyd and shaped him into the main man. Boyd had the looks, style and enough talent of his own, but from things Nicky's let slip over the ten years or so that I've known him, Boyd knew in his heart of hearts that he wouldn't have made it without Nicky's backing or blessing. They were chalk and cheese, but I believe they respected, even loved, each other. Boyd's death devastated Nicky, and it showed in his music. After *'Nowhere To Go'* and against the wishes of their fans, the group disbanded. Nicky and Phil had been the Makeweights before Boyd came along, but after his death they were only ever going to be known as his backing group. It didn't suit either of them, so they opted out. Phil was in demand as a drummer, while Nicky went back to song-writing. He turned out a lot of soulful, ballady stuff. Some he performed himself and had a few chart successes. But Chrissie Kingsley, Joe Spearing and Debbie Milligan all made their names and reputations from his songs."

Her gaze locked with Stephanie's: an uneven contest. "I pale into insignificance beside her." Her voice was calm, resigned, but he heard her dejection, as if a lesson had been drummed into her from day one, something she'd never been allowed to forget. Blore had started off not liking her at all but felt sorry for her now he understood her predicament.

"She saw in Nicky a potential he didn't want to own up to. Her ambition could have put him right up there alongside the Beatles, Stones and Hollies. He did okay, but the ambition which drove him was all hers. Still, credit her with starting him on the road. They met at some village hop in the early sixties. She walked in with her fiancé and out with Nicky. And he never looked back until – well, until she was no longer there."

"She died suddenly, didn't she?" Blore asked. "An accident in the Bay of Biscay?"

"Must be more than fifteen years ago now. Some wild party where everyone was drunk or stoned, and she fell overboard. Nicky's never really recovered. Nothing and no-one could replace her."

She glanced towards him with a smile of pain. She was going to say more, but then they heard voices in the hallway. Royce and Whitlow were coming back. Either they'd found a lot to talk about, or Chas had been in the loo a heck of a long time.

Lorraine smoothed out her expression. "So what is it you do for a living, Mr Blore?"

"Er, well -." The sudden change of tack had thrown him, let alone the question. "I was a company executive: Farmilow's, the retailing chain. I –um, had a breakdown, only just sort of resurfacing now. And you?"

He guessed she understood what kind of a breakdown it had been, because she kept her tone light. "Oh, I keep myself amused in London for three days a week. I've got shares in a small chain of boutiques. My friend who runs them has decided to start a family before it's too late, so I fill in here and there, mainly in a buying capacity. Sometimes it can be fun and sometimes not, but it beats sitting around at home."

And anything's got to beat that, she didn't add. But she'd said what she had with a smile, even if, he suspected, it was only skin deep. Besides, Royce and Whitlow had just come back into the room, and it was necessary for her to keep up appearances.

"All set, then?" Chas sounded bright and breezy, but Blore recognised the note of command. They both knew they'd got as much as they were likely to.

He forced a grin and thanked the Royces for their time. Nicky and Lorraine smiled back and saw them to the door.

"I don't think you'll find what you're looking for, Mr Blore." Nicky's parting shot as they shook hands. "I'm sorry. But – well, it was a long time ago, and it belongs where it is – way back in the past."

"It's still something I have to do," he countered bleakly, stung because he already knew he was staring defeat in the face.

Royce grinned tightly and left it at that. So did Blore. He had to, because Whitlow was already gently hustling him back to the car.

4

Ginny Duggan lived a few miles away in the hamlet of East Stoke on the edge of the Berkshire Downs. Royce had given them a phone number and, as they were already in the vicinity, Blore called ahead on his mobile in the hope that she might agree to see them that morning.

She did, with a manner both open and pleasant which set Blore at ease. As they drove, Whitlow filled him in on a few details regarding the Duggans. Some of it he'd just gleaned from Royce, proving that he hadn't spent his entire absence in the loo.

Phil Duggan had passed away three years previously after a long on-off fight with bowel cancer. Surrounded by too many memories of his struggle, Ginny had sold their four-bedroom house for a small cottage a few miles away. Bobby Duggan lived with her. He was thirty-four now, a self-employed gardener by trade. Royce felt there was something not quite right about Bobby, reckoning he might be a manic-depressive. He was protective of his mother, as he'd been for Phil, to a degree bordering on obsession.

The cottage was tucked away at the bottom of a narrow lane: thatched roof, pink-washed walls, and roses and clematis swarming up the trellis which formed a porch around the door.

This aura of tranquillity was blown away by the man who snatched open the door to Blore's tentative knock. He was wild-haired, wild-eyed, painfully thin in dirty blue jeans and a white T-shirt bearing a screaming rock band logo, and far from welcoming.

"I know why you're here," he stormed. "Mum might be a soft touch, but I'm not, see? No way I'm having all that crap dredged up again, right? Dad's been gone three bleeding years, and none of it can matter now, none of it, d'you hear me? So why don't you just piss off back to where you came from?"

Hands appeared at his shoulders, intent on easing him patiently to one side; and a calm voice spoke in the wake of his tirade.

"Bobby, darling, I invited them here. You don't have to talk to them – I'll do that. Please let them come in, there's a love."

To Blore's surprise, Bobby allowed himself to be eased, shuffling across to allow his mother to come to the door.

In her late fifties now, Ginny Duggan was still an attractive woman, shoulder-length hair ash-blonde and an absence of make-up. She was plump and petite, dressed in a crocheted pink cardigan, long patterned cotton skirt and Jesus sandals. She wore a silver crucifix at her throat and a genuine smile of welcome. Blore made the introductions, and Ginny shook hands with them, her grip surprisingly firm.

No handshake from Bobby. Blore offered, was ignored: Whitlow didn't bother. But at least Duggan had the good grace to stand aside as Ginny led her visitors through into a small, low-beamed sitting room. Phil's memorabilia filled the far wall, gold and platinum discs, along with photographs of Phil with the group, with Ginny and a younger, smiling Bobby. A round gate-leg table took up one side of the room, three cosy, floral-patterned armchairs round the empty fireplace the other. But the room was in no way cluttered: above the mantel shelf hung the portrait of an empty cross, bright flowers strewn around its foot; while a Bible rested across the top shelf of a small corner bookcase.

Ginny indicated the chairs and offered coffee. The two men accepted the first, declined the second. She sat facing them, while Bobby stood insolently aside, flicking disinterestedly through a gardening magazine.

Whitlow took charge. "Before we begin, Mrs Duggan. My pal here explained over the phone why we were calling. I'm an ex-policeman, but you should know there's nothing official about this. You're not obliged to answer any questions."

Ginny hadn't stopped smiling: she looked almost serene. "Thank you, Mr Whitlow. But it's perfectly all right. Mr Blore explained his reasons over the phone. I don't see how I can help, but I'm willing to do so if possible."

Blore felt it was time he took over. "Thank you for seeing us, Mrs Duggan. I was sorry to hear about Phil. He was a talented and dedicated musician."

He nodded towards the range of images behind her. Phil at his drums, big, wide grin, thatch of dark hair trimmed to fall just short of shoulder-length, sequinned jacket, fingers gleaming with rings. Then Phil some years later, hair shorter, clothes plainer, a group of schoolboys sitting awestruck in a semi-circle around him. And later still, gaunt and not quite smiling, the cancer gnawing at him by now as, frail and preoccupied, he sat alone on a stone bench gazing out to sea.

"Thank you. At the end, Phil had, quite honestly, had enough. But he was prepared: we both were. I'd discovered the Lord and His promise of life. Phil and I talked openly about it, and he knew he was bound for a better place, where he'd be made whole again; and that one day we'd all be together there."

She seemed content to draw the line at that. Not for her the endless moping, such as the ongoing grief of Nicky Royce. Blore had observed the Bible on the bookcase, the flowers at the cross, Ginny's sense of peace. What a difference they seemed to make. But he couldn't throw stones at Royce. What was he himself doing now, if it wasn't moping?

"Phil was one of the best, wasn't he?" he went on. He'd had no need to mug up on that period. *Top of the Pops,* Radio One: he remembered it all so well. "The general consensus was that he could have fitted seamlessly into any late 60s or early 70s group."

Ginny shook her head. "He was too much of a family man to be a great success. Bobby and I were the things that mattered most in his life, and I thank God daily for that. After the Makeweights folded, Phil hitched up with a couple of groups, but within two years he was back to session work and through that found a new career writing manuals and teaching in schools.

"While it was Phil and Nicky, life was good. The Makeweights got by, earned a living. All that changed when Ned Hargreaves came along. He'd 'discovered' Boyd and, by putting the three of them together, proclaimed that he could make them great."

"Surely he succeeded?"

She smiled indulgently. "I'm sure Ned would have you think so. Boyd, if he were here, would say it was all down to him, with his voice, looks and boundless energy. In truth it was the three of them together, not forgetting Ned's irresistible pushiness. The songs were Nicky's. Boyd may have contributed here and there, enough sometimes to claim co-authorship, but they weren't *his* songs, they all had Nicky stamped indelibly over them. But Ned pushed Boyd, Boyd pushed the group, and Phil and Nicky remained loyal all the way through. They ended up as makeweights – ironic, huh? The group they'd created turned them into also-rans."

Blore had had enough background. He was keen to get down to the nitty-gritty: the events which had occurred the morning Boyd died.

"Why was Phil visiting Boyd that last morning?" he asked. "An appointment had been made, hadn't it?"

Ginny answered readily. "It was Phil who made it. He needed to discuss his future with the group. He'd heard rumours that Boyd intended to replace him with Sonny Ralston."

Blore knew of this. The media at the time had made little of it, judging it to be another of Neelan's booze- or acid-driven whims. There couldn't have been a worse choice than Ralston anyway. A manic performer with the emerging glam-rock groups Hideous Strength and Blonde Machine, he'd never stayed in any one place too long and had OD'd somewhere in Holland in the late 1970s.

But Ginny was continuing unbidden. "I know Phil was anxious about it. In his heart of hearts he must have known that he needn't have worried, because there was no way Nicky would have stood by and let it happen. It was simply one of Boyd's wacky, thinking-aloud ideas: the sort of thing he'd pronounce on days when he was bored. He'd certainly never have thought it through. Still, Phil couldn't rest until he'd had it out with him."

Blore stole a glance at Bobby, still sullen and compounding that by also looking bored. He'd abandoned the magazine and sat astride the arm of his mother's chair, contemplating the ceiling.

"Your son was with Phil at the time?"

"Yes. Saturday morning was when I always did our weekly food shopping, and Bobby hated that." She smiled up at him and tapped his knee. "Still does, don't you, pet? Anyway, as always, he wanted to be with his dad. I was confident Phil would leave him in the car when he was talking to Boyd – Boyd's language wasn't always what you'd want a child to hear."

Whitlow cut in. Blore noticed he'd been watching Bobby with interest, observing his apparent unconcern.

"What can you remember from that morning, Mr Duggan?"

Bobby turned to him with a look of contempt. "I was *six* years old, Grandad. Doubt if you'd remember much from that age, although in your case it'd be going back centuries."

"Bobby!" Ginny was scandalised, almost knocking her son from his perch as she leapt to her feet. "There's no call for that!"

But Bobby stood up too, faced them all without actually looking anyone in the eye. "Sorry, Mum," he mumbled, then added, presumably to the other two: "Sorry. But it's – well, memories of Dad, see? Raking it all back up. Can't we just leave him in peace?"

His mother put her arm round him, eased him down into the chair she'd just vacated and knelt beside him. "Dad's at peace, darling. He's happy now – in a place where we'll all be together one day."

Bobby seemed unimpressed, still wouldn't look at anyone. "So you keep telling me."

Ginny looked up at their visitors. "I do beg your pardon. He's still very cut up about it – absolutely worshipped his dad."

Blore took the lead. He could see Whitlow wasn't likely to, tight-lipped and frowning as he stared back coldly at Bobby. "I'm the one who should be apologising, Mrs Duggan."

Ginny smiled forgivingly, and Bobby accorded him a half-nod, letting the silence thicken before he replied. But the reply was a bonus Blore hadn't expected.

"I remember the girl running from the studio to a car – a white Mustang as it turned out. She had a bag swinging from her shoulder and this long knife in her hand. She jumped in, swung the car round and came screeching past us. She was all over the place. Dad must've thought she was trying to run us down. He pushed me flat against our car, bashed my head. I remember she'd dropped the knife on the ground. There was blood on it, though I didn't know at the time that it was blood. Then Dad whisked me up and put me in the car, told me to stay put while he went into the studio. He wasn't gone long, but when he came back he looked really strange, sort of sad and shocked. It frightened me. I kept on: "Dad, is someone dead? What's the matter, Dad?" But he wouldn't answer me.

"He drove me along to Mr Royce's – I was bawling my eyes out by then – left me and went back there. Mr Royce gave me crisps and lemonade and let me watch something on the telly. There were a lot of comings and goings – loads of police. Some time later, Mum came along and fetched me home. Dad never got home for ages."

"Phil and Nicky were devastated," Ginny went on, as her son's narrative spluttered to a halt. "It was a great shock to us all, but it hit them extra hard, particularly Phil, because he'd found the body. Nicky was hopeless.

He kept mumbling, "Oh shit, if only Stevie was here." He simply couldn't cope."

"Stephanie Royce?"

"Yes. She'd gone up to London on the train, shopping, like she did about once a month. Of course, this was long before the days of mobile phones, and Nicky couldn't contact her. He tried phoning one or two of her usual haunts, but to no avail. She only learned what had happened when she got home that evening. She would have been a tower of strength, always so focused and purposeful. The boys were useless."

Everything tied in: Blore hadn't really expected otherwise, even though he'd hoped. They thanked the Duggans and took their leave. Bobby saw them to the door. He was still sullen: he was probably always sullen, but he'd calmed down since his outburst.

"So what's this all about?" he asked, eyeing the two men shiftily. "I mean, you some sort of journo? Or are you – " he addressed Whitlow's feet " – writing your memoirs?"

Blore came in quickly, dreading any sort of response from the lugubrious Chas. "I knew Anita Mead. I suppose she's –well, on my conscience. I don't think she was a killer, and I want justice for her."

"So it's your mission in life to prove her innocent? Must be a sad life."

Blore looked up sharply, biting back any retort he might have made. Duggan was openly sneering, but his last remark had hit the bull's-eye. *Yes, it had to be sad.*

57

"Best give it up, chum." Bobby's voice was suddenly level and his tone, strangely, not unkind. "Justice has already been done. I was there, and I won't ever forget it. I saw her drop the knife. It was covered in blood. Believe me, she did it all right."

★★★

He drove Whitlow home. Neither of them said a lot. The end of the first day of his 'investigation', and what had he achieved? He dared not ask Chas's opinion, because he feared what the answer might be.

When he pulled up outside Whitlow's home, a stark-looking, elderly bungalow on the corner of a cul-de-sac in Kidlington, Blore wondered aloud and tentatively about the next day. He'd arranged to visit Suzy Steller at her place down in the New Forest. Was Chas up for that?

The reply was a dry chuckle. "Yeah, I would've liked to come along. But I forgot to mention there was a message on my answer machine this morning. I've got to go up to the John Radcliffe, see some consultant. He wants to discuss the results of these tests they carried out. I should imagine he's discovered the old ticker's not so good – I had problems a year or two back. Dare say he's planning on wheeling me off to a nursing home for the rest of my days."

Blore started to make sympathetic noises, but Whitlow waved him to silence.

"Get away. I'm not at death's door yet: haven't felt better in a long while. But in any case, you're unlikely to need my help in getting the once-lovely Miss Steller to talk. Might need insurance, though. I've heard she still puts it about."

Blore allowed himself a wry grin. He didn't think there'd be much chance of Suzy Steller coming on to him. He felt about as desirable as an old ashtray. Or an empty glass.

But he knew he'd miss Whitlow's input and, yes, his company. He thanked him for tagging along that day. "I appreciate it. I mean, you don't have to help me."

The ex-DS shrugged indolently. "Gives me something to do, Jerry lad. Anyway, I'm still of the opinion the time'll come when you'll hit a brick wall and go no further. Someone needs to be around when that happens to dust you down and dole out the Elastoplast."

They said goodbye, Whitlow wished him luck for the following day – "You'll need it" – and Blore drove off. On his way through Kidlington, he remembered his fridge and freezer were bordering on empty and stopped off at Sainsbury's.

That was a mistake: the place was heaving, everyone purposefully manoeuvring well-laden trolleys in an effort to reach a checkout with minimum delay and get the hell out of there. Blore, forced into going with the flow, took a corner too sharply and hit an oncoming trolley head-on.

"*Shit!*" That wasn't Blore.

"I'm really sorry – ." That was. So was bracing himself for the verbal onslaught to follow, something along the lines of "Why don't you watch where you're going?" Only fruitier.

None came. "Ah, Mr Blore. Forgotten your 'L' plates?"

Blore dragged his gaze up to meet that of the woman behind the opposing trolley. She was tall, blonde, forties, features severe but not unattractive, a black leather jacket over a grey power-suit, business-like black heels.

"Oh, Inspector McCallum. Fancy bumping into you."

Mary McCallum scowled. "Just fancy. But I happen to live out this way, and even coppers have to eat."

His escaping glance raked the contents of her trolley: frozen this, frozen that, half-a-dozen bottles of plonk. Just a guess that she lived alone.

"I'm sorry. I didn't mean -."

Her face lapsed into a quick smile. "Forget it. I'm a grouchy cow. Long day at the office. Listen, the queues at the checkouts are a mile long. Fancy parking up and having a coffee?"

"Oh, right. Well, okay. But my treat – I insist. You've had me to put up with too."

McCallum's grin was feline: she'd go along with that. But her manner had changed. Just as he'd examined her purchases, she'd done the same with his, only less obtrusively. She must have guessed he was a recovering alky.

They parked the trolleys. Blore got the coffees and brought them over: hers an Americano, his a watery decaf.

"So how are things going?" He caught a hint of sympathy in her tone.

"Let's just say they're going."

"Hope I didn't land you in a hornets' nest when I sent you along to Chas Whitlow?"

So *that* was the reason for the sympathy. Who said coppers didn't have a conscience?

"No, he's been most helpful."

"Life's full of surprises."

"Although that doesn't mean he's not an acquired taste. I mean, he's made it clear he's not your greatest fan."

McCallum laughed. "Poor Chas. You could have knocked him down with a feather when they told him his new boss was a woman. He'd been Tom Arnison's skipper for years, and they'd been cosy. You know, man to man in a man's world – that sort of guff – a couple of really starchy old farts. Then Tom retired and Geordie Doyle took over: a different style, although Chas seemed to get on all right with him. But the job was already starting to change: technology was taking over, which made Chas and a number of others uncomfortable. Doyle got promotion and moved on, and I came in. For poor Chas, that really was the last straw. It must have felt like the job was piling insult after insult upon him.

"It's not that he wasn't good at his job. Just that he wasn't good around women, particularly when he learned he was going to have to take orders from one, and I wasn't going to let him piss me about. The minute the package was offered, he took it. Can't say I was sorry, but he wasn't a bad guy. For a long time I had him pegged as an old woofter, but he was just old school. No, older than old school. The Way We Did Things In Those Halcyon Days, according to the gospel of St Thomas Arnison."

Blore's turn to smile: a long time since he'd done that and been genuinely amused. "So what was it with Arnison?" he asked. "I mean, Chas should get top marks for loyalty. He chewed my ear a couple of times today for making what he thought were derogatory comments."

"He would. In fact he worshipped the ground my fabled ancestor trod. It was way before my time, and all the old-timers have gone now, but it seems Chas had a reputation for being difficult, never likely to rise above Detective Sergeant. A problem with booze too." She flicked Blore a wary glance as she said this, but he let it pass.

"Anyway," McCallum went on, "when Arnison arrived, he tamed him, kept him in line. Tom had a reputation as a man you didn't cross. He had family problems: his wife left him, and a son or daughter – I forget which – had had to be put in care. Arnison lived for the job and was good at it. He demanded the same commitment from everyone on his team. He must have struck a chord with Chas, because he turned him into a pretty decent skipper."

As Blore took all this in, Whitlow became more human in his estimation, and later he wondered if that was why she'd told him. But the lecture was over as far as the inspector was concerned. She set down her cup and pushed back her chair.

"Should have thinned out by now. I'd better be off. Early start tomorrow – as per. Thanks for the coffee, Mr Blore."

"Thanks. I –er, do believe there's something, you know."

She smiled again, indulgently now as if they both knew he was simply hoping against hope. "Fine. But don't raise your hopes too high. Oh, and don't tread on any toes, okay? I've enough on my plate."

He watched her go. *Nothing there. Don't raise your hopes. Justice already done.* Everyone was saying the same. And Blore, that man of perpetually low self-esteem, couldn't for the life of him see how he was going to change their minds.

But he was certainly going to try.

5

Blore set off early the next day, having arranged to be with Suzy Steller by ten. She'd told him she'd have to leave for London by midday, as she was involved in a West End play. So he was on the road by seven in an attempt to beat the jams on the A34.

Steller's country hideaway was exactly that. Called 'The Haven', it was buried deep in the New Forest down a narrow lane and even narrower drive. The house was 1930s' style, rendered in white with various oblong boxes tacked on to it, an architect's nightmare; or dream, depending on the architect. There was a rooftop terrace, so that Suzy and her guests could gaze over the rims of their champagne glasses and the tree tops for views of Lymington, the Solent and the Isle of Wight.

Suzy was leaning on the terrace rail as Blore chugged up the drive in his quietly rusting ten year-old Maestro. She cut an imposing figure in a billowing white trouser suit, outlined against the pale blue sky, her mane of corn-gold hair chased by the autumn breeze.

He parked beside a sparkling pink Mercedes and began to extricate himself from the car. She was downstairs and out of the front door before he'd succeeded, hands outstretched in greeting, as if she was welcoming an old friend.

Chas would have said it was because he was something in trousers, but after the po-faced reserve of Lorraine Royce and open distrust of Bobby Duggan, Blore would have replied that it was just nice to feel wanted.

Suzy Steller's blondeness was of the renewable variety, and she'd been liberal with the make-up, but at least she never lied about her age. She was fifty-two now, still with a good figure despite, or probably because of the usual enhancements, still a stylish dresser, though wobbling slightly in four-inch stilettos.

She'd come to prominence in pre-Boyd days, firstly as a leggy model in the early days of the mini-skirt, then as eye candy in TV game shows, Carry On films and their ilk. Post-Boyd, she'd graduated to lightweight, near-the-knuckle porn stuff. The *Melody Sweet* TV series of the mid-1970s was a prime example: a female spy spoof in which Suzy cut an appealing damsel-in-distress figure in skirts up to her midriff. Every heterosexual male on the planet had yearned to rescue her.

Today a welcome didn't come near it. Blore offered a hand, which she clasped lovingly, and the next he knew she'd latched on to his arm, wheeled him round and marched him through the open front door of the house.

He wasn't able to get a word in edgeways either: what a lovely day for October, glad you managed to find your way here from Brockenhurst, loads of people get themselves *hopelessly* lost; and terribly sorry about having to scoot off to London this afternoon, not being rude but the *play*, you know, in our second week *and* a new farce, and the cast are all lovely and interact so well, we're *determined* to make a go of it...

In polite half-listening mode, Blore allowed himself to be steered down an echoing, cavernous hallway and up a wide, curving staircase where everything, even the stair carpet, screamed white, and the walls were peppered with silly little daubs in softwood frames. It all screamed money too, as was the intention; but whispered emptiness and loneliness, and he felt a twinge of pity for this garrulous, bouncing woman who clung so possessively to his arm that it was starting to feel numb.

She led him through a bedroom, hers, he presumed: huge, circular bed, deep pile carpet, wardrobes lining two walls, all, as he might have guessed, in white. Out on to the terrace Suzy had lately vacated, and she pitched him into an armchair, took the one opposite and edged it closer to his so that their knees were almost touching. Then, with a dazzling smile, she picked up a tinkly little bell from the bistro table beside her chair and deployed it vigorously for a good ten seconds.

"Well, Mr Bourne, I have to say your phone call stirred a few memories, Poor Boydie. D'you know, life's so darned *full* that I sometimes forget all about him? Are you writing a book, Mr Bourne? I'll get some coffee brought up – *if* I can get some service." She rang the bell again.

"Er, it's Blore," he corrected her.

"Sorry, lovey?"

"My name. It's Blore, not Bourne."

"Oh, do forgive me. Well, why bother with surnames? I'm Suzy, and you – you mentioned it on the phone – Gerald?"

"Jeremy, But I prefer Jerry."

"Ah. I knew a Jerry once. Or was it Gerry with a 'G'? Oh, who cares? So *there* you are at last. You took an *age*. Thought you might be trying to make yourself look beautiful – though you'd need every age known to man to bring that off."

She was right there. As she'd been banging on about names, Blore had gradually become aware of a figure sidling through the french windows on to the terrace. The arrival was a pasty-faced, unsmiling woman of indeterminate years, dressed in a shapeless grey uniform, her dark hair twisted into a severe bun.

"Beg pardon, mum. Cleaning the silver. Didn't hear your visitor knock."

"He didn't, Waters. Anyway, you're as deaf as a post, so he'd still be knocking. This is Jerry – Mr Blore to you. He's writing a book – aren't you? – about when I was the young, desirable Mrs Neelan."

"Right, mum. All those years ago."

"Thank you, Waters. Now hobble off back to your lair and make us some coffee. And bring some *decent* biscuits, nothing that you've been taking bites out of. Go on. Scoot."

Waters turned unhurriedly and disappeared the way she'd come. Suzy beamed at Blore. "Miserable old fossil. I inherited her with the house and didn't have the heart to pension her off. So much for compassion. S'pose I saw her as Mrs Danvers to my Rebecca, although at my age I'd be cast as Danvers. Talk about ironic. Now, Jerry. Enough wittering, and down to business. I've simply *got* to be in London by mid-afternoon, darling, so I'll get right to the heart of the matter. This may come as a shock to you, but I'll make no secret of it. I was responsible for Boyd Neelan's death."

She was right again. Blore, steeped in gullibility, was shocked. He supposed it was just what he wanted to hear: if someone else was guilty, that had to mean that Anita was innocent. But common sense kicked in, as he saw that Steller, ever the actress, was smiling creamily at the effect she'd just achieved.

"Well, Boyd and I, you know, it wasn't exactly a marriage made in *heaven.* More by the media – which is about as far from heaven as it's possible to get. The teen mags simply thrived on us: *Fab, Rave, Honey* – the whole lot. Of course, it was Boyd they wanted, with their predominantly little-girl readerships. I got hate mail for months. You'd never believe some of the things his so-called fans threatened to do to me. And as for name-calling, parts of their vocabulary even made *me* blush. Here, have a butcher's at these."

He'd noticed the pile of photo albums beside her chair. She heaved up a couple and pitched them in his lap. He began to leaf through them. Wedding pictures by the yard: Boyd tall and elegant – in three years Ned Hargreaves had ironed out all his gawkiness – in leprechaun-green suit and grey top hat; Suzy, blonde, demure and utterly desirable in white mini-dress and matching boots, smiling sweetly over the top of a gigantic bouquet of red roses.

Then press clippings in their hundreds: *'Suzy's No Ordinary Makeweight'; 'She's Top Of Boyd's Pops'.* And photographs of the guests: Nicky Royce in white tie and tails, his hair lustrous and shoulder-length, with Stephanie in a long, flowing dress, striking and stately on his arm; Phil Duggan smiling awkwardly, Ginny calm and serene beside him, beads dangling from her neck and a garland of flowers round her head; and a bemused-looking toddler – Bobby – in velvet suit with bow tie wildly askew, clinging to her hand. Other celebrities and big-wigs – the number of guests had run to hundreds – mingling, grinning, pouting, drinking. Relics of a bygone age: even Blore, something of a sixties' buff, had forgotten who some of them had been. A line from one of Boyd's songs flitted across his mind: *'I'm gone, I'm long time gone, so don't stay here.'*

There were cigarettes and a lighter on the table. Suzy offered, Blore declined, and she lit one for herself, puffing reflectively away for some moments as she launched a straggling trail of smoke over the terrace rail.

"But it was always going to come to grief. So much pressure on us both, each with our careers to make; and so many hangers-on, all with dollops of conflicting advice and fair-weather friendship. I was getting offered parts left, right and centre, so I was often away filming, sometimes abroad. And if I wasn't around, Boyd wouldn't need much encouragement to stray."

Waters came shuffling back with a silver tray bearing coffee pot, crockery and a plate of chocolate biscuits, each one intact as far as Blore could tell. The whole thing rattled as she set it down on the table before them, earning her an incisive glare from her employer.

"Would you like me to pour, mum?"

"No."

"Will there be anything else, mum?"

"Oh, Waters, just go, will you? And stop trying to come across as the maidservant. Mr Blore's not convinced, and you know only too well how I feel."

"Very good, mum."

She departed at snail's pace and Steller, barely able to contain her exasperation, busied herself in dispensing coffee and offering biscuits. She cast a suspicious sidelong glance at the french windows before, finally reassured that Waters wasn't eavesdropping, she lit another cigarette and continued.

"The day he died, I'll admit I flipped. I mean, I just *lost* it. I phoned him in the morning from London. He told me he was expecting Phil Duggan for an urgent discussion, hoping that might be enough to put me off. Some hopes. I told him in no uncertain terms that I was dropping by, because we needed to sort matters out once and for all. I'd heard that good-for-nothing little tart was putting word around that Boyd was ditching me in her favour. I mean, as *if*! She was the last in a long line of them, each one as predictable as the last. Housekeeper, my backside! Doubt if she could boil an egg. Well, I'd had enough, and it was time to do something about it. I'd been filming down on the south coast. *Beach Balls And Candy Floss* – oh, Jerry dear, I'll forgive you if you don't remember it. It turned up late on Channel Four the other week. God, I looked good. Isn't it a pity we have to grow old?

"Anyway, I was determined to have it out with Boyd. I stormed over there and pitched her out on her ear – my, didn't she run – then told Boyd exactly what I thought of him. He put up a fight but quickly saw reason and agreed to dump her in order to save our marriage. If he hadn't, he knew I'd go straight to the papers, and guess who they'd have sided with? Boyd already had a terrible reputation as a love rat. So once I'd issued my ultimatum, I left. She had no money and nowhere to go. They quarrelled, she flipped, stabbed him and did away with herself out of remorse. And I'd set it all in motion."

She paused, mainly for breath, ground out her cigarette and picked up her coffee cup. He sipped at his, uncomfortably aware that she was carefully scrutinising him over the rim of hers. He had no option but to meet her gaze; did so reluctantly.

She seemed amused by his coyness. "C'mon, Jerry. Why all the interest in this? You've got to be a journalist. Or is it that you're writing a book? Kind of first-time effort, trying to make it big?"

He struggled to answer, knew he wouldn't be able to fob her off with a lie; but knew too that he couldn't divulge the whole truth. *Because I was a hopeless drunk, because I chased my wife away, the only woman there'd ever **really** been, and because somehow, in some shape or form, I have to try to make reparation, and it has to start here.*

"There was a – drink problem," he admitted falteringly. "I – well, it's behind me now. I'm getting back on track, and she – Anita Mead – you see, we knew each other well for a few years, through school, and I'm certain she was no killer. Call it a guilt trip if you like, because perhaps that's what it is. But I want to get justice for her…"

Suzy was about to answer, shifting impatiently in her seat as if it was hurting her not to be actually talking, when her attention was drawn to a movement behind the french windows.

"Oh Christ, Waters, what is it now?"

"Mr Grayston, mum. Will he be staying tonight? I mean, will you be wanting me to make up the room?"

"No, Waters, you brainless old crone, of course he won't be staying *tonight*. I'm going to be up in London anyway and won't be back until late Saturday night. Mr Grayston'll come too, if I'm lucky. Now stop spying on us and shuffle off back to your cauldron."

She watched, seething, until she was satisfied that the woman had taken herself off. Blore read the papers. Barry Grayston was a rising young actor, currently appearing with Steller in the West End. Twenty-five years her junior, and there'd been rumours. But Suzy had never been one to deny those.

He waited for her attention again, waited on her answer, knowing what to expect. What he hadn't expected was the genuine sympathy, the regret behind her war-painted lashes. She smiled wanly.

"You're wasting your time, Jerry dear. You see, she did it all right – signed, sealed and delivered. Okay, so you knew her well. You were lovers, and you reckon because of that you knew her best of all, and you're saying she wasn't capable of doing what she did. But how can any of us know what we're capable of until the moment arrives? A crime of passion, the papers said. I think that sums it up.

"So you can write your book or salve your conscience or whatever, Mr Blore. But let me say this. It happened nearly thirty years ago. It's back deep in the past, dead and buried, like your Anita and my Boydie. They're gone, and we should forget them. I'm sorry if that sounds harsh, but I think you know what I mean."

How could he not know? *And Boyd lives on, immortal through his music, still admired, mourned, feted, people wondering what he might have achieved. While Anita is pushed to one side, his murderer, a name to be reviled if it wasn't so forgotten. And here am I, Annie, your last hold on life, last chance of justice. Just me. Only me. You deserve better.*

In his dejection, Blore was already pushing back his chair as she was speaking. He could see she pitied him, and it made him feel worse. He stuttered his thanks for her time, but she wouldn't let him go. She led him back through the house, and he followed meekly.

Suzy talked all the time, pointing out this and that. The furniture was modern, the rooms uncluttered, but the whole place was a shrine to Suzy Steller, photographs dappling every wall in gilt and silver frames. Suzy in this or that film, hugging this or that celebrity, always grinning, laughing, living life to the full. What had she said? That there were times when she'd almost forgotten Boyd? *But who was Boyd?* She'd not only outlived him by nearly three decades, she'd outgrown, outmanoeuvred him. And the scenes she pointed out to Blore now were clips from a busy and successful life, jigsaw pieces of her triumph.

He wondered if she'd read his thoughts, for finally she turned to him, eyes glinting with some reflection of that triumph.

"Not bad, eh, for some little waif brought up and bullied in a rotten orphanage? I've *worked,* Mr Blore. And by that I don't mean I've spent half my life flat on my back. I've put in one *hell* of an effort, and it's me who's got me where I am."

Blore wound himself up for one last try: he couldn't bear to leave with nothing. Suzy tolerated his persistence, but she'd lost interest a long time back: hence the guided tour, the paeans of self-praise.

"I don't know what happened afterwards. Oh yes, Phil Duggan found the body. He went along to Nicky Royce, and between them they came to the conclusion they should call the police. Honestly – nice guys, but what a pair of ditherers! I was out of there well before then. I was in one hell of a flap – Nicky said afterwards that my language was foul. But, shit, Boyd and Anita between them had got me wound up like a spring. In fact, as I drove off, that little whore emerged from the bushes dragging on a spliff. I nearly mowed her down – and for Boydie's sake, I wish I had.

"Anyway, I came back early evening – six o'clock or something, because I said I'd be back for his answer. I doubted whether he'd have kicked her out by then and was ready for another set-to and, well, you know what I found."

They'd reached his car, and Suzy turned towards him, her expression more serious than it had been at any time during his visit. She laid a hand on his arm, not without tenderness.

"Mr Blore, nothing's changed except the time. I'm sorry."

He was grateful for her sympathy, even though he could have lived without it. She didn't wave him off. By the time he was driving away, she'd already gone back inside.

6

T *hose times were good: the only time in my life that I felt truly alive, the only time I came close to feeling like any other human being.*

No, wrong. I felt like a king. And then, at the height of that blissful and wonderful feeling, she was gone. Taken. Spirited away.

I was left to pick up the pieces of my life. And as I look back down the years, I realise that's all there's ever been: pieces.

★★★

The phone rang early evening, liberating him from a mindless TV programme. He couldn't have said why he'd been watching it in the first place, but he was still numb from his meeting with Suzy Steller and tired from the journey. He answered it, hoping it wasn't yet one more cold call offering him some impossibly free holiday.

"I take it she let you keep your trousers." Whitlow, his tone Sahara-dry.

Blore chuckled. "That was never going to be a problem. But no result otherwise."

"You sound surprised. You didn't ought to be."

"Not surprised. Disappointed. I – well, just hoped it might have been different."

"With the trousers?"

He chuckled some more. Chas being therapeutic? How many more surprises? "With the result. And what about you? How did it go at the hospital?"

"Pretty well if you like being given the verdict that you're a walking time-bomb."

"I'm sorry."

"Don't be. He's only a consultant: what does he know? It won't stop me carrying on in the same way. Come on, lad. Let's change the subject."

"Okay, let's get back to where we were. I just get the feeling there's something hidden here. Something someone's not telling."

He didn't know why he'd said that. Something hidden? *Dream on.* He knew he was snatching at straws, fearful of coming up against the brick wall Whitlow had predicted.

Blore sensed the other man's shrug. "Guess it could be they're all just hacked off with you."

"Oh, thanks."

"No, hold on." Whitlow's tone was reasonable. "You've got to understand how they feel. Everything's resolved, everyone's getting on with their lives, then thirty years down the line along comes some amateur who rakes it all up, maintaining his girlfriend was innocent when she was as guilty as sin."

"Thanks again. You're a hell of a confidence builder."

"Only trying to put it in perspective. So – where to now?"

"Ned Hargreaves is about all that's left. I phoned him when I got in. He can't see me until the day after tomorrow."

"That'll be something to look forward to. He'll be only too pleased to discuss theories with you, and you can bet your boots he'll be looking for some angle that'll benefit him."

Blore nodded. He'd only enjoyed a brief conversation with Hargreaves but reckoned Whitlow was spot on. The man had come across as unctuous and eager to please. A mite too eager for Blore's liking.

"Neddy's been there, done that and got the T-shirt," Chas went on. "Journo, manager, DJ, author. Boyd Neelan was his ticket to millionaire-dom, until he got dead. Ned's been a busy boy and milked Neelan's memory for all it's worth – maybe more. But he's never had it so good as when Boyd was alive. Day after tomorrow, you say?"

"That's right."

"So how about filling the gap with 'Seabirds'?"

"The guest house? Mardon Regis?"

"The very same."

"Thirty years on, I should think the landlady's long dead."

Whitlow laughed. "Ethel? Don't you believe it, chum. She's still with us and right as ninepence in the top storey. I checked."

"You *checked*?"

"Just thought I'd help you see this out. Then we can all get a bit of peace. She's expecting us late morning, by the way."

Blore couldn't believe it, left momentarily speechless.

"I'll pick you up then, shall I?" Whitlow went on. "Eight o'clock sound okay?"

"Yes – sure. And thanks. Thanks a lot. Er, let me give you directions."

Eight o'clock on the dot an ageing red Escort pulled up in front of his house. Chas was at the wheel, wearing a smile. Blore couldn't help wondering if he'd experienced some sort of Damascus Road conversion overnight. If so, bring it on; although somehow he doubted it. They kicked off with the usual small talk, but Blore quickly brought the conversation round to what was for him the burning issue.

"Listen, Chas, you didn't have to check up on Ethel Robey, and you're under no obligation to chaperon me. Done and dusted, you said. Are you maybe thinking there's something in this after all?"

Whitlow's smile faded as he concentrated on driving. When he answered some moments later, his voice was a low growl.

"I'll come clean with you, Jerry lad. It doesn't sit easily. Every instinct tells me to forget it, to walk away, 'cos we're wasting our time. And yet – well, I'll go so far with you. We'll talk to Ethel, and you can talk to nerdy Ned – you're on your own there, 'cos he hacks me off big-time. If nothing's jumped up and smacked me in the face by then, I'm going back to my pipe and slippers."

Blore was amazed and pleased in equal measure, and Whitlow took advantage of his silence to give him a bit of background on Ethel Robey.

She still lived at Seabirds, now a 'hotel' in modern parlance. Her son and his wife ran it now, for Ethel was well into her eighties. Whitlow had interviewed her personally at the time.

"Arnison sent me down there, 'cos he had his work cut out interviewing the Neelan set, while at the same time fending off the media and the demands of the top brass. It suited me: I was all for a day at the seaside. A day was all it was, as things turned out."

Mardon Regis had been a popular resort since the turn of the century. It boasted a long stretch of sandy beach, one of the south coast's longest piers and the famous Esplanade Gardens with their winding gravelled walks, profusion of flowers and shrubs, bowling-green lawns and bandstand.

The summer season had ended a few weeks previously, but the promenade still boasted a smattering of visitors, the sea-front cafes doing a healthy trade. Seabirds Hotel lay beyond it, where the coast road turned inland, its view of the beach blocked by a row of kiosks and gift shops which lay opposite.

It was a sprawling, pebble-dashed bungalow, sleek with a recent coat of paint on its frames and sills. A short, jovial man in his fifties, Ethel Robey's son, answered their ring at the door.

"Come in, gents, do. Ma's expecting you. Quite fired up, she is – don't get many visitors these days. And if it's something to do with donkey's years ago, as she tells me it is, there'll be no stopping her."

He led them through a hallway and dining room redolent with the stale aroma of countless cooked breakfasts to a door marked 'Private'. Behind it lay a small, tidy sitting room with a large TV set in one corner and some ancient but comfortable-looking armchairs gathered round it. In one of these, hemmed in by a sewing-box, parked-up zimmer frame and coffee table camouflaged with books, magazines, newspapers and magnifying glass, sat an elderly lady.

She looked up on hearing them enter. Even though the room felt warm, she was swathed in a baggy Shetland cardigan. But her iron-grey hair was newly permed, her face lit up at the sight of them, eradicating many of its lines, and her eyes held a keen sparkle.

She wagged a finger at Whitlow. "Ah – I know that face. The policeman who called here. Come in and take a seat, young man. And your friend too."

"Mrs Robey." Whitlow crossed the room and delicately shook the hand she offered. "So good to see you again. As I said over the phone, it's about that business of Anita Mead – the Boyd Neelan murder case from all those years ago." He jerked a thumb over his shoulder. "This is Mr Blore. Anita was a friend of his." He paused while Blore leaned across to shake hands. "We're looking at the case again to see if we can discover any new leads. As you've remembered, I worked on it at the time. Detective Sergeant Charles Whitlow, now retired."

"Ah, of course, that's the name. Whitlow. I've been puzzling over it all night. It would have come to me eventually though, I'll be bound."

Whitlow was grinning almost boyishly and flashed Blore a mischievous glance. "I thought I'd better accompany Mr Blore in case you needed someone to jog your memory."

"*Me!* Huh!" The old lady glared at him indignantly. She knew it was a wind-up, because she hadn't lost her smile. "I should hope not, young man. I may have trouble getting about these days, but you'll find there's very little *I've* forgotten."

Ethel's son had remained at the door, watching this exchange with amusement. "She certainly enjoyed the media coverage," he chipped in. "Queen of Mardon for months afterwards, weren't you, Ma? Never had it so good."

Ethel swung round imperiously. "Get in that kitchen and fetch these nice men some coffee, Albert, and stop jawing, do. And they reckon it's us women who're always gassing."

Admonished, Albert gave a despairing shake of the head. "Right, Ma." He grinned at the two visitors. "No prizes for guessing who's still boss around here."

"None," Ethel confirmed. She waited until her son had left the room, then fixed her attention on Blore. "Pull your chair a bit closer, young man. As I said, there's nothing wrong with *my* memory. After Mr Whittall here had phoned, I set myself to thinking. I'd finished my library books, and there's nothing *ever* on that television. Back-handed gift from my Albert, that."

She settled herself back in her chair and stared resolutely at a point some two feet above the heads of the men facing her.

"It was about this time of year, wasn't it? Late September. It was out of season and, as I recall, I had just one elderly couple staying here. Lovely old pair, but I'm bothered if I can recall their names to mind. Still, no matter: they'll have been dead for ages. 'Seabirds' was smaller then, of course. Albert and Josie built on to the back and side of the place ten years ago. Tut, that boy with his grand ideas. Still, they don't run the place too badly between the two of them, I must say.

"Anyhow, I thought right away that there was something odd about that young miss. Booked herself in as 'Susan Starr' and paused over the register as if she had to think what name she'd put. Tut, I can see her now. A dress with red-and-white hoops, and so short you'd scarcely believe it. No luggage either, apart from one of those canvassy shoulder bags. A typical miss, too: she wouldn't look at me direct-like. Still, doubt if she could see me with all that hair in her eyes. They were all the same, those girls. Could have been so pretty if they'd dressed in nice summer frocks and done something with their hair. Almost as bad as today: black this, black that and all that war-paint.

"But, you know, I could tell right away that this one was upset about something. Made it clear she just wanted to be left alone. I had a feeling then it was something to do with some man, and she wanted away from him.

"I offered her some supper. Lovely stew I'd done, but madam said she didn't want any. Still the old people lapped it up, bless their hearts. I asked her if everything was all right. She said she was tired – she'd had a long journey. I knocked on her door later to see if there was anything she wanted. But the door was bolted and there was no answer, so I guessed she was sound asleep.

"'Course, I heard it on the news that night about some pop star being murdered and them wanting to interview his housekeeper. She didn't look like any sort of housekeeper, so it never struck me at the time that it might be her. Next morning they showed her picture. A bit blurry, but it was her and no mistake. By then, though, she'd gone."

Albert came back into the room bearing a tray of coffee and biscuits. He started to fuss over it, but Ethel impatiently sent him on his way. She was into her tale now and wasn't prepared to be interrupted. So Albert quietly withdrew, and Whitlow acted as 'mother'.

Once that duty was done, Ethel resumed. "She came into the dining room in the morning, had a bit of breakfast all nervous and distracted-like and just said hello and what nice weather to the old people. But something wasn't right. 'Course, if I'd chanced to see the news – but I was in the kitchen cooking breakfast. That old pair *loved* their fry-ups.

"Anyway, once she was finished she got up and started out of the room. As I recall, I was bringing the old people their toast. My, but couldn't they tuck in! Well, madam walked past me, then happened to look out of that big dining-room window through there and gasped. I looked round, and she came back over and drew me aside. "Mrs Robey," she said. "There's a man over the road by those shops. I think he may call here, and I really don't want to see him. Please, if he calls, just send him away – say I've left or something."

"Goodness me, she was all a-quiver. I tried to calm her, promised I wouldn't let nobody in. She pointed him out to me. He was standing there smoking. It seemed like he was watching the place, but of course he might have been waiting for someone. Just across the road he was, in front of that parade of shops you'll have seen before you turned in here."

"Can you remember what he looked like?" Blore asked. He was leaning forward in his seat, as alert to his own expectation as to the tightly grinning scrutiny of Chas beside him.

"Can I *remember*?" Ethel smiled and wagged an admonitory finger at Blore. She nodded towards Whitlow. "This young man asked me, oh, a whole host of questions all those years ago, and I wouldn't be surprised if I weren't giving you exactly the same answers today.

"Well, he was one of those hippy types. Really bushy dark hair, droopy moustache and dark glasses, even though it was a dullish morning. He wore one of those – Afghan coats, I think they were called – always looked scruffy – and a bright green neckerchief and tight white trousers that seemed to balloon out at the bottoms. Real hairy monster, he was."

"Did he call?"

"No, he never did. I stayed there in the lounge, switched on the radio after the old people had gone and watched and waited. Well, that's where I heard about it on the news, and it only occurred to me later that she was the girl they were looking for. He stood there a good fifteen minutes by my reckoning, turning and walking along a bit, gazing in all the shop windows. There were lots of people milling around by then, but I never lost sight of him. Anyway, eventually he seemed to get fed up and walked off towards the prom. I watched him out of sight.

"I went to let her know, and *that's* when it occurred to me she might be the girl they were looking for. I knocked on her door, thinking I might just have a quiet chat and, if it was her, persuade her to give herself up. But there was no answer. The door was unbolted, so I went in. She was gone – the window left wide open.

"Well, I called the police then – and I shall rue the fact to my dying day that I never did so sooner. They found her dead in the river a few hours later, poor mite. I dare say she did kill this Boyce Needler. But I expect he provoked her, seducing the poor lamb with drink or drugs or some such."

"Was the man actually watching the house, Mrs Robey?" Blore asked tensely. "He couldn't simply have been a passer-by, or waiting by the shops to meet someone?"

Ethel shook her head decisively. "He was definitely watching the house. And for a fact she knew him from somewhere."

"She didn't mention a name at all – give some clue?"

"No, my dear. No name – nothing, I'm afraid."

Blore continued to probe, but Ethel had nothing more to tell them, and it was Whitlow who finally drew stumps, thanking her for her time and for agreeing to see them at such short notice.

"Oh, it's a pleasure, young man. I don't get out a lot, and it's so nice to have company. Albert's not much fun, as you'll have gathered."

They shook hands. Her frail fingers lingered on Blore's, and she gazed up at him with a sympathetic smile, her eyes bright with sadness, with a message he didn't wish to understand.

"I hope you find what you're looking for, dear."

Albert saw them out, grateful for their visit for his mum's sake, and as the door closed on them Whitlow asked Blore if he wanted to visit the spot where Anita's body had been found.

He shook his head. He'd been there before, of course. Not around the time it happened, but in recent months, after he'd come back to life. Once had been enough to enable him to visit and revisit it time after time in his unquiet mind.

A high bridge over the River Mar, on a remote country road shaded by an avenue of trees. A fisherman had found her late in the afternoon of the day she'd left Seabirds. She was lying face down in the reeds, having jumped from the bridge and drowned.

Three miles out of Mardon: she must have walked there, because none of the taxi companies had a record of her. Might even have hitched a lift, but despite appeals from the police no-one had come forward.

What had gone through her mind in the hour or so it would have taken her to reach the bridge? Had she even known where she'd been going? It seemed unlikely. But she'd needed to get out of Seabirds, hadn't wanted to go back through the town; so this road would have been about her only option.

Blore had stood on the bridge a few months back, gazed down on that tranquil scene, the water skittering over the stones, the tall reeds swaying gracefully in the breeze, the willow branches caressing the surface of the water. Weeping willows.

And he'd been sad. Sad for the life she'd been denied, the life spirited away. And for the life he'd led, the scattered pieces he was scurrying around desperately to pick up. Knowing they had only ever been pieces.

Blore brought himself back to the present, leading the way back to the car with an air of purpose. He had other things to think of now: no longer Annie's suicide but, as it appeared to him, the real possibility of her murder.

He realised Whitlow was watching him, a sly reconnaissance. There were no flies on Chas, he had to allow him that: for Chas knew what was in his mind, knew what was to come. And Blore, for his part, knew what reaction he'd get from Chas.

They drove away. Whitlow, grinning smugly, began to chuckle as the heavy silence lengthened.

"Well?" he said at last. "Going to share what's on your mind?"

Blore was secretly elated. He didn't want Chas to know that, because he knew he'd quickly get slapped down, have the rug ripped away from under his feet.

"Mr Afro?" Chas prompted.

Blore took care to keep his voice level. Whitlow, of course, had known about this all along. He'd carried out the initial interview with Ethel Robey. So was this what 'didn't sit easily' with him?

"Mr Afro," he confirmed. "He could have killed Anita – seen her and followed her to the bridge, even picked her up and driven her there."

"Why should he?" Chas countered reasonably. "*She'd* killed Neelan, not him."

"But do we know that for certain?" Try as he might, Blore couldn't stop his elation seeping through: blood from a self-inflicted wound. "Is there some way Afro might have killed Boyd, then pinned it on Anita?"

"If we knew who Afro was," Chas stated tartly, "then we might stand a chance of answering that." Before Blore could react, he jabbed a finger at a road sign they were approaching. "I'm pulling into the lay-by along here. We need to talk."

No argument. But Blore couldn't help feeling an argument wasn't far ahead. He wondered if Chas was nettled by something he'd just said, something he'd alluded to. Perhaps he'd push his luck a bit further: anything for answers.

Whitlow brought the car to a halt, killed the ignition, waited. The silence lengthened, and Blore understood that it was down to him to break it. "What's the problem?" he asked.

"Listen." Whitlow sounded calm and controlled. "You've just been and got yourself a nice new theory. I could tell by the way you were nearly wetting yourself on old Ethel's sofa back there. Okay, have your theory and welcome. But understand this, Jerry lad. We can sit here till midnight and discuss every theory you can dream up, and I'll guarantee this: we'll have thought of it and checked it out at the time. Or at least started to."

Blore glanced up sharply. "Started to? What do you mean by that?"

"Tom Arnison pulled me off it. I was here happily investigating away, eager and willing to probe deeper into Ethel's story. But he pulled me out 'cos in his opinion as senior officer, it was all cut and dried.

"Okay, I've been through it time and again over the years and come to the conclusion that Tom was right. Let's play back over the scenario at Dreamfields: Anita rushed out and dropped the knife. There was blood on her hands. She took off in the car, which she later abandoned. They found blood on the travel rug where she'd wiped her hands, found it smeared on the steering wheel where she'd tried to clean it off with the rug. Neelan's blood. She came here by train, went to Seabirds to hide out, couldn't get her head together, ran off and topped herself through remorse. Crime of passion, lad. I told you so before."

Blore asked his burning question, knowing full well that Whitlow would have the answer ready. "But what about Afro?"

Chas shrugged. "Lad, Afro could have been *anyone.* Tom dismissed it as a ruse. Anita sussed correctly that Ethel Robey was suspicious. So she looked out of the window and picked on some poor Herbert who was waiting for his bird, pointed him out to Ethel, and while she was busy keeping tabs on him took the opportunity to slip away."

"And simply gave up on everything, went off and took her own life."

The bitterness in his voice registered with Whitlow, who spread his hands in a conciliatory way. "That's about the size of it. Can't you see that, Jerry? Or is it just that you don't want to see? 'Cos she had nowhere else to go. She'd killed her lover in cold blood on the spur of the moment. Who'd side with her over that? And what sort of turmoil do you think was going on in her head right then? I'm sorry, but I think Tom Arnison made the right call."

"But surely he couldn't gloss over everything like that?"

Anger had crept in among the bitterness now, and Whitlow reacted in the same vein. "Not like that, no," he snapped. "Not like *that,* 'cos he'd have chewed it over time and again until it felt right. He was a really thorough sort of guy. But there was pressure from above for a quick result. This was international news, and we were under scrutiny. Arnison had the Chief Constable on his back morning, noon and night. The murder of a world-famous pop star: the image of the whole country's police force would benefit from a quick clear-up. And as I said, we got the right result."

"And did Tom Arnison's reputation no harm at all."

Blore knew right away that he shouldn't have said that, but he'd given in to his frustration. Chas, however, didn't bite, simply threw him a sullen glance. "I'll pretend I didn't hear that. You didn't know him, didn't know the pride he took in doing the job right. He was a fine officer and a decent man."

Blore sensed the tension between them and gave in, knowing that he needed the ex-DS on his side. "I'm sorry. That was uncalled-for."

Whitlow nodded. "Apology accepted. Let's get back." He started the car and drove off, a tight smile tugging at the corners of his mouth. "You don't intend letting this go, do you, Jerry?"

Blore kept his gaze averted: the tension was still there, even if it was only in himself. "Probably not." But there was no 'probably' about it. He fully intended following up the Afro issue. He would do it with or without Chas, and Chas knew that.

They made good time on the journey back, making little conversation. Blore didn't think it politic to discuss the case further: it could wait. He suggested Chas stop off for a cup of tea before making for home. It was an olive branch, and Whitlow, realising it to be such, accepted.

Blore lived in the cottage where he'd been born and bred, a mile outside Witney: a grimy, two-up, two-down stone building, once with a thriving vegetable garden at the front. Blore had moved back in almost a year ago, after his mother had passed away. She'd done nothing with the garden in her last year of life, and he'd been disinclined to revive it. Instead, he'd strewn several tons of gravel over it, rendering it into a piece of waste ground where he parked his battered old car. Mum had been proud of that garden, as had Gran before her. For Blore, that seemed to sum up everything regarding the way he felt about himself. The industry and pride which had been their way of life left him lagging far behind.

As Whitlow drove through the gateway, Blore knew something was wrong. Mum had had a conifer in a large glazed pot outside the front door, a birthday present years before from her occasionally dutiful son. Now the conifer lay on its side across the garden path, the pot around it in shards.

Blore was out of the car before it had stopped and running towards it, turning as he heard Whitlow call his name.

Chas had wound down his window and was pointing at the driver-side front wheel of Blore's Maestro. The tyre was flat.

"Puncture?" Blore asked, as he made his way back there. He was always forgetting to check his tyre pressures.

Whitlow had got out of the car to examine the tyre more closely. "Sure," he replied. "The kind of puncture a sharp knife makes." He showed Blore where the tyre had been slashed, nodded down the garden towards the shattered pot. "And I doubt if that was caused by a gust of wind," he added.

"It's odd," Blore said. "Never have kids larking about up here. It's too far out of the town."

Chas grinned wryly. "You know, Jerry lad," he said. "I don't think kids had anything to do with this. I said to you last night that you were probably hacking certain people off. Is it just that? Or might it be that someone's got something to hide after all?"

7

Together they attended to the wheel. Fortunately the spare was in reasonable condition, and the change-over didn't take long. But Blore wasn't going to let Whitlow disappear in a hurry. He invited him indoors, made him a cup of tea, then drove into Witney for some fish and chips.

The wily ex-policeman had quickly spied an ulterior motive.

"You're not giving this up without a fight, are you?" His eyes twinkled, all traces of earlier annoyance gone. But the fish and chips were a big help: they'd only had a sandwich and a couple of Ethel's biscuits all day.

They washed down their meal with tea, Blore apologising that he kept nothing stronger in the house. Chas merely shrugged: he understood about that.

Blore had been busy with his thoughts on the short trip into Witney and back. "Ethel's an important witness," he reasoned. "She saw and described Afro. He hung around there for a long time and if he'd been waiting for someone, clearly he or she didn't turn up, because he was seen walking away *alone*.

"As I see it, he must have been someone Anita knew. Perhaps someone outside the Boyd Neelan set?"

"It would have to be," Whitlow agreed. "I'd got some way into my questioning before Tom reeled me back in. Afro didn't sound like anyone in Boyd's or the Makeweights' immediate circle of friends. So – supposing she knew him, where did Anita know him from?"

"I kept in touch with her for a while after she'd moved to London," Blore said. "Although it was the period before she hitched up to Neelan. It's something I can chase up when I go there tomorrow."

★★★

Fired up. Was he? Or was it simply a question of pain returning, that self-inflicted, utterly merited pain? Once Chas had gone, he sat alone in the gathering gloom and looked at the room around him: the armchair and sofa with the stuffing coming out, the scratched Welsh dresser and those Spode plates which had been given to Gran on her marriage over eighty years previously. He had grown up with it all: very little had changed or even shifted position down the years, sorry mementoes of his boyhood and young manhood. He'd grown up poor: he'd wanted to change that, *achieve* something, knowing that he'd have to work his socks off to get there. That, Blore supposed, had been his first mistake.

"Jerry honey, I'm splitting. I reckon it's now or never, so I'm off to the big, bad city. Fancy coming along? We could shack up together, see how it works out?"

Why had he said no? It was laughable really. "Annie, I want to make something of my life too. There's a junior management post coming up in the Birmingham store…"

Blore almost choked on his mineral water. Dear God –Birmingham! He'd let her walk out of his life and down the slippery slope to death within eighteen months of her leaving – and for Birmingham!

The irony was that he never got there. Instead he soon after obtained a similar position in the Oxford store, just a short coach or train journey from London.

"Sounds heavy, sweetie pie. And I'm goin' to miss you. But if you've got to go your way and me go mine – well, maybe we'll meet up again one day, who knows? Oh, but Jerry, maybe it's for the best. Your mum hates my guts, she reckons I'm a right little scrubber. And you – well, you're just a real nice guy. So you go ahead and make a success of things, and I'll try to do the same. Let's keep in touch. I promise I'll write when I've got a job and somewhere to stay."

And she kept her promise: she wrote. She'd found employment in Sacha's, this Soho night club and, right on, London was *swinging* and the people just, like, crazy, out of this world. She'd met this racing driver, that footballer, that film star – "and you'll never guess, sugar, never in a million years: *Boyd bloody Neelan*. I mean, who'd ever have thought it…?"

But that was the last letter he'd got. He went up there once on his day off. Just really to see where she was living, how she was getting on, take her out to lunch, and – real motive – see if they could somehow get back together, because things weren't too hot on the girlfriend front. The junior store manager taking on the might of the racing, sport and film worlds as well as one of *the* pop giants: talk about David and Goliath.

Because he had to admit it: he *missed* her. Life was getting to be all work, and he'd just got clear of his mum's apron strings. Totally against her wishes, he was renting a shoe-box of a pad off the Cowley Road and reckoned he ought to find someone to share it with.

Poor Mum, always trying to bring him up 'properly'. He'd never known his dad, and he sometimes wondered if she'd known much about him either: a shadowy figure rarely alluded to. Blore gathered he'd decamped with another woman years before. Mum had worked long shifts at one of the Witney mills, resourcefully ensuring there was food on the table and clothes to wear. As a child he'd had nothing, and only got money to spend when his gran had slipped him the odd shilling, or later when he was old enough to do a paper round.

Like it or not, they'd been on a par socially with Anita and her boozy mum; but as far as Mrs Blore was concerned, they were streets apart. *"You're surely not going around with that Mead girl, Jeremy?"* Bless her, she'd had forty fits – would have had four hundred and forty if she'd known what they got up to. *And yes, Mum, Annie was mad, bad and dangerous to know, but we had great fun together. And yes – I **miss** her.*

But Annie hadn't been at Sacha's. It was down a steep flight of steps deep in Soho: small, dark, stinking of stale beer and staler flesh. A surly cleaner in shirtsleeves – he might even have been the manager – sent him on his way.

So he'd trawled along to her flat, to some dismal street in Balham, a grungy bed-sit up two peeling-wallpaper flights.

She shared it with three other girls. It was the middle of the day, and all three were there: one sprawled on the floor smoking pot and floating way out somewhere, the others mini-skirted and bra-less, waggling their breasts at him unashamedly, high on flirtation and daring.

"Say, Wends, here's a real groovy guy. But he's looking for Annie."

"Shit, what a disappointment. She's not at home, honey bunch. Out somewhere with her latest dreamboat. He's stinking rich and drives a Lamborghini."

"Where'd you park your Lamborghini, groovy guy?"

"Hey, Shirl, he says he came up by train."

"Another disappointment. But we can make it right, babe. See, Annie won't be back till late – or probably very early – and you can kind of bunk down with us if you want."

"Yeah, we're cool and friendly, and there's lots of nice things we can think up to help pass the time."

He tried to smile, forcing it with all his might; tried flirting back, but his heart wasn't in it. They were too cool, too easy, and he just wanted out of there. And the sweet sickliness of the tripped-out girl's joint pervaded the room and offended his prim little up-and-coming *bourgeois* soul.

But that wasn't all, not the whole story. Because in those few alarming moments, he'd known for a certainty that the two worlds claiming Annie and himself were totally different, light years apart. And right there and then, he consigned her to the past that he was outgrowing: because he'd lost her.

He never went back there, and she never wrote again. He never knew, never cared if the stinking rich dreamboat with the Lamborghini had been Boyd Neelan. In any case, Boyd wasn't many months down the line.

Neither was death.

★★★

His second glimpse of Sacha's came thirty years later. That October morning, fittingly grey and wind-swept, Blore studied it from across the street. It was a hair salon now, gleaming with chrome and brilliant-white linoleum, windows shrieking with posters of glossy girls in immaculate hair creations, the atmosphere bright, airy and gossipy inside.

That was about it for memory lane.

Granucci's, the restaurant where he and Ned Hargreaves had agreed to meet for lunch, wasn't far away. Blore had come up from Oxford by train, reluctant to face the drive into London. He'd tried Chas again first thing, but the ex-DS had refused point blank. "I'll only end up throttling the little ponce. No, Jerry lad, you're on your own. But give us a bell when you get back – I'd be curious to know what nerdy Ned has to say."

He didn't mind Granucci's: pseudo-Italian surroundings catering for a self-important, endlessly yattering clientele. It was lunch-time, and the restaurant was a popular place. He recognised several faces: once-upon-a-time celebrities working overtime to be celebrities again, and wannabes who ached to get there but never would. It seemed a fitting venue at which to meet Ned Hargreaves.

Ned had reserved a table, and Blore was shown to it. Nobody seemed to mind his crumpled, hang-dog appearance, indeed it looked to be the fashion. They probably had him down for a City geek on a day off.

He was halfway through his first Perrier when Hargreaves made his entrance. He weaved between the tables the way Blore remembered Andy Williams had done in his synthetic 1960s TV show, glad-handing all and sundry. Some saw him off with a quick greeting and false smile, others either stared blankly or ignored him completely.

He walked, beaming, over to where Blore sat. The first thing Blore observed was how short he was: probably no more than five-three or four. He couldn't be far off sixty but was fighting it gamely, his skin taut and shining, a testament to Botox, eyes bulging, brown hair with swathes of grey drawn back in a pony tail. He wore a maroon shirt, a wide white tie dappled with yellow blotches which might have been egg yolk, tight blue jeans and crocodile shoes with a small heel. Blore guessed it had all come off designer pegs, but didn't think he'd swap the rumpled look.

They shook hands and rattled through the usual chit-chat: Blore's journey across town, weather, news headlines, all break-the-ice stuff. Hargreaves' voice was light, cultured, rather twee, as if he'd been to a posh school. Blore was sure it was contrived: in his Neelan research, he recalled reading that Ned had been a Barnardo's boy from a working-class background.

They mulled over the menu. Hargreaves selected something with spaghetti which sounded positively evil, the Italian pronunciation tripping daintily off his tongue; Blore stuck with pizza. Ned had a large glass of Montepulciano; Blore kicked off his shoes and went for a second Perrier.

"Now, Mr Blore – may I call you Jerry? Please, call me Ned – everyone does. You explained over the phone that you were researching into dear Boyd's unfortunate demise. I –um, take it you'll have read my book?"

The Boy From The Emerald Isle. It was over twenty-five years old, couched in a twinkling style which, having heard him speak, Blore could readily associate with Hargreaves. But no-one could deny that it was hands-on, a decent read. He'd gleaned more background from it than any other source. "I have indeed."

"It flutters in and out of print whenever there's some sort of Boyd milestone to celebrate. The definitive work, I'm sure you'll agree."

"No-one can accuse you of not knowing your subject."

"Well, I was there, wasn't I? And no-one knew him quite like I did: manager, mentor, friend, confidant – part of the scene. I believe I've painted a sympathetic picture. Some of the trash which appeared in the years following his death didn't pull any punches but didn't bother much with the truth either. Boyd wasn't all bad. Sure, he did booze, drugs and women: there were few of his standing who didn't. In my humble opinion, that so-called wife of his was – is – far worse. But naturally the blonde hair, baby blue eyes and oh-so-perfect and well-travelled body pulled the wool over the media's eyes."

Catty. And nothing humble about it. Hargreaves took a long pull at his wine, and Blore took advantage of the pause to get in a word.

"Some of the other accounts reckon Boyd was going to ditch Suzy in favour of Anita Mead. I take it you didn't subscribe to that view?"

Ned pulled a face, giving the impression of a constipated toad. "Anita was a lovely girl, but she was dizzy. She never stopped spinning."

Blore nodded: that summed up Annie.

"Jerry, who knows what Boyd promised her or any of them? These girls were all empty-headed little chits. He made them feel good with the attention and money he lavished on them. Most came from poor backgrounds, and Boyd's generosity simply blew their minds. They were all pretty, well qualified in the usual departments and couldn't see he was after one thing only. Not until he dumped them: usually, I may say in his defence, with a generous parting gift of money.

"The day it happened I was here in London, negotiating with the powers that be for an open-air concert in Hyde Park the following spring. It had worked for the Stones in '69 and would have been a supreme showcase for Boyd and the boys. But, as you'll have read, and I go along with the general opinion, Suzy blasted in that day and handed Boyd an ultimatum. Bullied him, if you like, in a desperate bid to save their oh-so-sacred marriage.

"Mark my words, Jerry, it was all a performance for the glossies. But Boyd gave in, as I'm sure he had to, and when he told Anita she went ape. After all, he'd probably promised her the earth, and in her innocence she believed him. Anyway, they quarrelled, fought, and Boyd was fatally stabbed. I don't believe for a minute that Anita meant to do it."

Blore nodded again: he seemed to be doing a lot of that. It signified concurrence, which was the last thing he wanted. So he tried for a reaction: anything to jolt Hargreaves out of his creamy complacency.

"I should imagine it turned your world upside down," he said. "Boyd was one of *the* big stars, and all of a sudden he was gone."

Ned looked suitably affronted. He could see where Blore was heading. *All those future earnings reduced to nothing at a stroke.*

"It was a shock. Of course it was. But more than that, it was a tragedy. I mourned the poor dear boy for *months*. After all, I'd got him to where he was – *created* him, you might say. And to find it spirited away in one senseless moment -!"

The claws were showing again. But Blore wasn't going to antagonise the little man by taking umbrage. He needed him on his side. He wondered briefly what Ned had mourned most: Neelan or the sudden loss of income. In the years that had followed, he'd taken every opportunity to compensate for the second by exhaustively preying on the memory of the first.

"So you didn't get hassled by the police?" Blore asked.

Ned shrugged, a Quasimodo-like hunching of the shoulders. "Oh, they came and asked questions, mainly about how things stood between Boyd and Anita. The investigating officer and a scowling sidekick. But all was speedily resolved when that witless girl chose to take her own life."

Blore had to suppress a grin: no prizes for guessing who'd been the scowling sidekick. Hargreaves took advantage of the pause to signal the waiter for another glass of wine before returning to the offensive.

"And she took her own life, my friend, because she'd murdered Boyd."

Ned couldn't have underlined it better if he'd had a marker pen. His gaze scanned Blore's face, clocked the disappointment, the hopelessness.

"But clearly, Jerry, you'd like to think otherwise. Why is that? She was, I presume, a former girlfriend? After all this time, it sounds as if you're suffering from a misplaced sense of guilt."

Guilt again. Blore, swallowing down the last of his pizza, nodded thoughtfully. Hargreaves was right, of course, as was Chas. He wanted justice now, because he couldn't be bothered with it then: because he'd lost her, let her slip away. *After all this time.* But it did matter – to him: something he could get right, redressing in some small part all the things he'd got wrong – Annie, Cassie, himself. *Something I have to do.*

And now, finally, he had something on the plus side, because at least in Ned Hargreaves he'd found a listener. He explained to Ned that, even though it was too late to change anything, he'd known Anita well and couldn't believe she was a killer. He was searching for a new angle; and now he believed he'd found one.

He knew right away that Ned was hooked. Whitlow's words came back to him: *something that'll benefit him.* Hargreaves was a vulture: it was down to the long-ago journalist inside him. He saw an opportunity here, and there was no way he was going to spurn it.

"It was an issue," Blore went on, "that DCI Arnison didn't follow up at the time – pulled his sergeant off it, in fact."

"Ah." Ned smiled, the compression of his pudgy lips making him look more toad-like than before. "The great Arnison. Or was it Arsey –son? Lugubrious sort of chap: unlucky in love, I suspect." He sat back in his chair, hands resting contentedly on his pot belly as he waited for Blore to deliver.

Blore obliged. He told Hargreaves about Ethel Robey's evidence: the watcher at Seabirds on the morning Anita had died. Was Afro in any way connected with Anita? She'd met a lot of men at Sacha's in her pre-Neelan days, undoubtedly slept with a few of them. Even more than a few. He described Afro. Ned had been on the scene in those days. Might it be anyone he remembered?

"Sacha's." Ned pondered over his double espresso. "Yeah, Jerry, remember it well. Strange little chap who ran it – a Turk, I believe. Half a mo' and the name'll come to me. Ah – got it: Remzi. That was it. Bit of a voyeur, as I recall. Died of a heart attack a couple of years later, spying on his dancers in their dressing room."

He wasn't so sure about Afro: the hairstyle and clothing had been common to practically every other early '70s young male.

"I thought of getting myself an afro once," Ned chuckled. "Can you imagine it, eh?" Blore smiled politely: it didn't bear thinking about.

"I'll check on it for you anyway," Hargreaves promised, as they swapped mobile phone numbers. "You should see the clutter at my pad. Memorabilia, they call it. My old auntie would have called it junk. I'll have a trawl back through the photographs and memories, Jerry. As I say, I was part of the scene back then. The description could fit a dozen people I knew, and that's just for starters. However, I'm inclined to agree with your policeman friend: it's not one of Boyd's circle. Must be one of Anita's *beaux*."

Ned took the opportunity to slip away at that moment, He'd spotted Amanda – hadn't seen her in *ages*

– must ask her about the new show. Oh, and there was Justin. The new hair suited him. Must check out that rumour about the comeback album.

He shook hands distractedly and scurried away. Justin blanked him and Amanda, trapped, looked as if she desperately wished she were somewhere else. Gradually the persistent Hargreaves was sucked into the madding lunch-time crowd.

Smartly leaving Blore with the bill. Nice one.

★★★

Blore hadn't been up to London in a while and dawdled around in the afternoon, dipping into the National Gallery and Imperial War Museum. Back at Paddington, he found himself in the tail of the rush hour, and the Oxford train was pretty full. Even so he managed to grab a window seat and buried his nose in an early edition of the *Evening Standard*.

"Excuse me, is this seat taken?"

"No, go ahead."

"Thank you. Oh!"

He looked up on hearing the note of surprise in the speaker's voice. He recognised her with a jolt and guessed surprise was too mild: try shock, even horror. He wasn't feeling too clever himself.

Lorraine Royce hovered over him, trim in grey trouser suit and heels. She'd already been halfway into the seat when she'd clocked him, so to move away then would have been an obvious snub. Besides, there didn't appear to be any vacant seats in the vicinity.

So she sat, and an awkward silence kicked in. It suddenly seemed a hell of a long way back to Oxford, although he guessed she'd get off at Didcot. Even so, he was still going to have to make a stab at conversation.

"Good day in London?"

They uttered the phrase simultaneously, stared at each other for a gormless moment and laughed. She was attractive when she laughed: good teeth, her nose wrinkling prettily. He guessed he didn't have the same effect on her, which was hardly surprising.

"A working one for me," she said. "I'm helping run my friend's boutiques while she sits back and enjoys her pregnancy."

He felt a bit of a twerp, because she'd told him that the other day. He nodded dumbly, grateful that she was too polite to remind him.

"And you?" Her tone was light and, he suspected, teasing. "Carrying out inquiries?"

"I had lunch with Ned Hargreaves."

"I see." She didn't sound greatly impressed, and he could understand how Hargreaves might have that effect on people. "I expect he had plenty to say for himself?"

"Let's say he kept the conversation flowing. Er, I take it Nicky doesn't see much of him these days?"

"No, thank God. Once Boyd Neelan was off the scene, Mr Hargreaves decided it was time to move on. Nicky was never going to be a glamorous enough prospect for him, even though he's made a decent living through his songs. Besides, Ned couldn't wait to cash in on the biography he was writing. I wouldn't have put it past him to have had the first sheet of paper in his typewriter within minutes of hearing of Boyd's death."

Neither would Blore, having met him. But he was saved a reply as Lorraine shifted in her seat and fixed him with an earnest stare.

"Mr Blore? Can I be direct?"

He'd never thought for a moment since setting eyes on her that she was likely to be anything else. He nodded permission.

"This friend of yours, the ex-policeman. What's his interest in this? Does he think there may be something which didn't come out in the original investigation?"

Blore wondered about mentioning Afro and quickly decided against it. *It doesn't sit easily,* Chas had said. It was better left, at least for the time being.

"I think he's just tagging along out of the kindness of his heart," he replied. "He's tried to put me off a couple of times. I guess he's just hanging in there to gently reel me in once we've exhausted all the possibilities."

"Then why -?" She was staring at him frankly; and yet, he felt, not without compassion. "I'm sorry, I'm being direct again."

"Fire ahead."

"Well, what I mean to say is, why are you going on with this? It all took place so long ago. What can you hope to achieve after all this time?"

It was a good question, and he wasn't sure he had an answer. *Peace of mind? A purpose in life?* Both came close. Ned Hargreaves had come closer still: *a guilt trip.*

"I want to clear Anita's name. She was my girl, you see, before she met Neelan, and I can't believe - ."

"But why now? Why not right after it happened?"

"Because I'd walked away from her by then. It's only now, when I've had time on my hands and I've been able to think. You see, I've been away."

"In prison?"

He guessed she was being polite, pretty sure that she'd sussed him out when they'd spoken the other day. He scored her a point for that; and another because she was waiting patiently on his answer and not looking or sounding as if she felt the need to distance herself from him.

He grinned awkwardly. "That's pretty close. I – well, I was an alcoholic. Still am technically, I suppose."

It was becoming easier, living with it. They'd said it would. And he was glad he'd said it, because it was as if a mask had been snatched away, and better still by his own hand: a lying mask of pretence. He wondered darkly if there might be others; and if he might ever be able to tear them all away.

"I'm sober now," he went on. "I intend to stay that way. I found her photograph the other day, you see. We'd been very close: a year at school, a couple afterwards. I'm looking for a new slant on this, because there's just no way I see her as a killer."

"I can't say best of luck." Her manner had thawed: the warmest he'd experienced in their two meetings, but still lukewarm and aloof. "Nicky's not a well man himself. He's been for tests, and things don't look good. He seems to be heading down the same road as Phil Duggan."

"I'm sorry."

She shrugged. "You needn't be. He's not. He's positive, philosophical, and he says I must be too. But, well, things'd be better if he didn't have to put up with all this being dragged into the open again."

"I understand. But I hope you understand that it's something I have to do. It's a conviction, not a whim. As I said, we're following a new line of inquiry. I hope we'll be able to leave both you and Nicky out of it."

"It would be appreciated." Lorraine glanced out of the window. "Anyway – my station. I must go. It's been nice talking to you, er, Jerry."

"You too. And thanks."

"What for?"

"For listening. It's helped me."

"Oh. Oh, good. Well, I'll say goodbye then."

The train ground to a halt. Doors swished open and shut. As the train moved off again, Blore settled back in his seat, his thoughts racing. He was hopeful of leaving the Royces out of it, because he felt sure that Ned Hargreaves' offer of help would bear fruit.

And that there'd soon be another name in the frame.

8

He was right on both counts. Ned phoned Blore early the following morning.

"Jerry, my friend. And a very good morning to you. May I report that I've worked my way through endless NMEs and the like and arrived at the conclusion that your man may well be a musician by the name of Chip Harper."

"Who?"

Ned chuckled. "Afraid you'd say that. Bit of a 70s journeyman. Got himself a reputation for smashing up guitars on stage. Or at least he tried to. It worked for The Who and others, but Chip was never in the same league."

He went on to list the groups Harper had appeared with, among them Hairpin Bend and Deadly Ernest, both whom had appeared at Sacha's in late 1970 and the first half of '71 when Anita had been working there. There was a definite chance they might have met.

"What was his real name?"

"Byron, I think. But no-one called him anything other than Chip, because he carried one on his shoulder wherever he went."

"Sounds a nice man."

"Shall we say he had a bit of an attitude?"

"Whether or not, I suppose I'm going to have to talk to him. Any idea where he might be?"

Again the chuckle. "Try prayer or a medium, Jerry. The poor love's been dead ten years: speed overtook him. But all is not lost. Another of his groups – he changed them as regularly as his underwear – was the Strawberry Eclairs."

"Never heard of them."

"Few people have. They enjoyed a couple of very minor hits before fading into obscurity."

"And they performed at Sacha's too?"

"Oh no. They didn't surface until '72, the year after Boyd's death. Chip Harper played lead guitar, and they had a drummer you may have heard of. Name of Phil Duggan."

Blore nearly fell off his seat. As a new line of inquiry, this was turning into something else, and there was no way he might have seen it coming. The smug silence on the far end of the phone suggested that Hargreaves was relishing the mayhem he'd unleashed.

"I see," Blore said at last, not really sure what he was seeing, but certain of one thing: doors were opening. And he wondered why they'd never been opened before.

"Indeed," Ned returned smoothly. "Something for you to chew over and pursue, Jerry my friend. And of course if anything looks like coming of it, I'd be obliged if you'd think of me first. About time I stormed into print again."

Blore promised he would, and as soon as he'd ended the call phoned Whitlow. He'd contacted him as requested the previous evening to relay the main points of his initial meeting with Hargreaves.

Whitlow, as expected, had been snide about that, but the latest revelation gave him something to think on. He hadn't foreseen it and grudgingly assented to go along with Blore. "But you ought to bear in mind that it might lead nowhere," he warned. Even so, he couldn't dent Blore's mood of growing expectancy.

They agreed they should talk to Ginny Duggan again, preferably without her son in tow. Guessing he must work somewhere, Blore phoned and asked if they could drop by late morning. Ginny seemed to sense that they'd prefer to speak to her alone. She reassured Blore that Bobby was out on a job at present – he was a self-employed gardener – and wasn't expected home until the evening.

She opened the door to them dressed in the same long skirt and sandals as on their previous visit. She wore the same smile of welcome too and had coffee and home-made scones awaiting them.

Blore liked her. In everything he'd read and all he'd heard, she came across as a genuine and gentle person. There was a fragility about her: clearly she'd loved Phil deeply, and his passing had hit her hard. But he sensed too an inner strength and guessed that she was more than compensated by her faith and its promise of life to come. For a wistful moment, he wondered if he could ever own such reassurance, such peace. It was a twinge, a fleeting ache: he let the moment pass.

He didn't like having to question her again, raising issues which had to be painful because they brought back memories of Phil. And as they sat and talked, he could almost sense Bobby's presence, his twisted antagonism hanging over them like a curse.

Ginny remembered Chip Harper. She'd only met him on a couple of occasions and hadn't warmed to him. The Strawberry Eclairs had formed in 1972, almost twelve months after Neelan's death, and Ginny was certain Phil hadn't known Harper beforehand.

"They wouldn't have had a lot in common. Phil joined the Eclairs because the Makeweights didn't wish to continue without Boyd, and quite honestly we needed the money. But the rest of the group were heavily into drugs, and Phil wanted no part of that. I think they simply wanted to trade on his name. It bought them a couple of minor hits, but within six months Phil had had enough and left. They sank without trace after that."

Blore apologised for returning to Duggan's visit to Neelan on the morning of his death.

"You thought it was one of Boyd's whims – replacing Phil with Sonny Ralston. Might there have been some basis to it? Had Phil and Boyd quarrelled at all?"

She shook her head. "Not that I recall. Although there was one occasion, when I'd just got home after taking Bobby to school. I was surprised to find Boyd waiting for me at the house. I could tell he was high on something and didn't want to let him in. He'd always been flirtatious with Stevie Royce and I – well, really with any vaguely attractive woman who crossed his path. There was a real tension about him, and I found I hadn't guessed wrong. He started going on about free love, and how love made the world go round – those time-worn clichés. How Phil was out and Suzy off filming, and how we could be real consolation for one another.

"I sent him packing as gently as I could. In his defence he didn't lay a finger on me, and when he saw he was cutting no ice he simply got back in his car and left. I told Phil all about it when he got home, just in case Boyd happened to mention it and put his particular spin on it.

"Phil was livid. I don't think I've ever seen him so angry. He was all for going round and giving Boyd a piece of his mind – and this from Phil, one of the least confrontational people on the planet. I calmed him down, begged him not to take it any further. It had just been Boyd on one of his whims – he always had them when he was drunk or high – and all that had suffered had been his ego."

"How long before Boyd's death did this happen?"

Her quick glance told him she knew where he was heading. "Just a few weeks. But Boyd carried on as if nothing had taken place. Which, when you think about it, was right. It had been merely a whim, and a crazy one at that."

"Might it have been Neelan's way of getting back at you?" Whitlow asked. "This idea of his to replace Phil?"

But nothing was capable of disturbing Ginny's air of serenity. "Maybe, who knows? Phil worried about it for days before his meeting with Boyd, but in my opinion he needn't have. Even if it had been likely to happen, there's no way Nicky would have put up with it. Boyd might have been able to replace Phil, but he would have limped along without Nicky." She smiled fondly at the recollection. "Poor Boyd. He had great talent but just didn't know how to treat people. He'd suffered an horrendous childhood, abused by his father and uncle, and ran away to England when he was just sixteen. He was one of the lucky ones: he got the breaks. I'm sorry it ended the way it did. But I take comfort from the fact that he's beyond pain.

"And so is Phil." Her hand went to the cross at her throat. "No more suffering. I'm so glad. Phil was an ordinary man – you had to know him to understand how ordinary. He became disillusioned with the pop scene, often recalling with Nicky the times when they'd been just the Makeweights. Life had seemed so simple then: the boys lived for and feasted on their music, and Stevie and I were their only groupies. Phil may have had his most prosperous years with Boyd, but they were increasingly unhappy and unstable."

Ginny went on unbidden to speak of Phil's devotion to their son. "Bobby idolised his father and was devastated when he died. I believe that for years he clung to the unreasonable hope that a recovery was possible. But I knew there could only be the ultimate form of healing. And Bobby's means of coming to terms with Phil's death has been to act as my protector. I apologise for his behaviour the other day. He means no ill."

Whitlow accepted this graciously and got to his feet. Blore had no more questions anyway and followed his lead. He sensed an air of finality in Ginny's handshake as she held the door open for them; and in her parting words.

"But it's that poor girl I feel most sorry for. One moment of madness, and it cost her her life. Still, I pray that she's at peace now."

There was a pub in the village, and the two men adjourned for a ploughman's lunch. Blore's suggestion, and it won him an amused glance from Whitlow.

"A pub, Jerry? This a change of heart?"

"A bite to eat, Chas. Washed down with a glass of water. Although I'm happy to stand you a pint."

"You're on."

Blore's real motive was less to do with food than with having somewhere other than the car to sit and discuss what was on his mind. Chip Harper was turning into an obsession, and he badly wanted Chas with him on this.

"Chas, don't you feel it's significant the way everything fell apart for Phil Duggan after Neelan's death?"

Whitlow looked puzzled. "How do you mean?"

"Well, Boyd seemed to have got it into his head that Duggan was too low-key. What if it was more than a whim? What if he was actively trying to replace Phil? Maybe Phil and Boyd quarrelled, Boyd got killed, Anita witnessed it and ran off, and Duggan and Harper tracked her down and silenced her?"

Chas held up a hand. "Just rein 'em in there, boy. You're assuming Phil knew Harper before they hitched up with the Strawberry Eclairs. Ginny sounded certain that wasn't the case."

"But he might have kept it from her. You have to admit it's not out of the question and easy enough to prove. Ned Hargreaves - ."

"Oh, you bet *he* could," Whitlow cut in harshly. "If there's a link to be found, that little weasel could be guaranteed to turn it up. Either that or fabricate it. In any case, Anita had the knife and dropped it at the scene."

"The *boy* said she dropped it," Blore pointed out. "He was six years old, and how do we know his father might not have influenced him? Okay, I'll admit it's wild. But it's worth a look, if only because I'm convinced Chip Harper's involved there somewhere."

Whitlow was shaking his head. "You're in danger of running amok with this, Jerry lad. Here's a word of caution. Harper's only in this according to Ned

Hargreaves. Added to that, he's dead and can't speak up for himself."

Blore stared back, stunned. "What are you saying? That Hargreaves has his own axe to grind? When I met him - ."

"When you met him he was slippery, the way he's always been. Just bear it in mind if nothing else, Jerry. You'll be able to guarantee one if not two things. First – as is likely – Ned sees something in this for himself."

"And second?"

"That he's trying to cast suspicion in a certain direction."

"Whose?"

Chas shrugged. "That's not clear as yet – if it's the case. But I'd put nothing past him. He'll have some old scores to settle. He was the devoted manager, for sure. But Neelan was getting bigger all the time: the main man, Jerry, the *only* man. If he could contemplate replacing one of the best drummers around, why not a nerdy little tick who was always getting up people's noses? Six years on, Boyd was an international star. He could pick and choose his manager. Did he *need* Ned? It's just a thought."

A hell of a thought too, but Blore was still hot on the Harper question. He didn't want to be deflected and was gearing himself up to argue further, when they were interrupted by the ringing of Chas's mobile.

Chas answered it, listened to what was being said, his expression stony with annoyance. His replies were brusque and monosyllabic. Eventually he snapped off the phone, dropped it in his pocket and stared hard at Blore.

"Your friend the inspector," he said accusingly, as if it was all Blore's fault. Which, thinking about it, it probably was. "You can put it to her in person about reopening the case. 'Cos she's requested we drop by and see her, as of right now. And from her tone, I don't think it's for tea, fairy cakes and a girlie chat."

9

Whitlow was right there. Just as he was when he advised Blore not to break any speed records getting back to Oxford, because McCallum kept them waiting in reception for over twenty minutes.

Finally she shoved head and shoulders through the swing doors and beckoned them, stomping ahead up the stairs, her high heels clacking petulantly. When they entered her office, she was already at her desk and indicated chairs for them. Blore recalled his meeting with her at Sainsbury's the other evening. He supposed he'd glimpsed her off duty then, but she was undoubtedly on duty now. She looked formidable, the last word in not suffering fools gladly. And there were no prizes for guessing the identity of the fools.

However, when she spoke her tone was surprisingly light. "So what have you two been up to these last couple of days?"

Blore looked at Chas, whose face might have been carved from granite. Knowing the way he felt about McCallum, Blore guessed he wasn't going to take the lead in case he said something he'd regret, so it was down to him.

She didn't give him the chance, instead answering her own question. "Because whatever it is, you've been upsetting people. And I'm afraid I can't have that."

Rattled someone's cage, in other words. Blore took heart from it. Chas was still doing his effigy impression, so he took a deep breath and waded in.

"Who's upset, Inspector? Someone who's worried that we're getting close to the truth?"

Mary McCallum leaned back in her chair, swaying a little from side to side as she considered her reply. A smile, dangerous and predatory, spread slowly across her face. She stopped swaying abruptly and leaned forward on to the desk, fixing Blore with a hostile glare.

"A deputation, Mr Blore: Mr and Mrs Royce and Robert Duggan. They came to see me earlier this afternoon. As you may know, Mr Royce is far from well, and your inquiries are an unnecessary extra burden. As for Mr Duggan, he wants you to stop harassing his mother."

"But that's ridiculous," Blore protested. "Nicky Royce I can understand, and I've assured his wife I'll try not to trouble them again. And in fact we've only just come from visiting Ginny Duggan. She didn't give any indication -."

"Clearly her son doesn't know about your latest visit, then. And the complaint's from him, not her."

"So what's he got to -?" Blore began angrily; and stopped. Because he knew where Bobby was coming from, and it meant that he was vindicated. It came back to Phil Duggan's link with Chip Harper. Was there something in it after all? Something Bobby had feared they'd bring to light sooner or later?

But it was just as well he'd stopped, because McCallum's voice cut in, the tone icy.

"Mr Blore, this isn't a police matter – yet. I've told them they're under no obligation to say another word to you. But I'm strongly advising you to leave them alone as of now – before I make it a police matter. I dare say all your questions have done is resurrect the same old answers and reopen the same old wounds."

Astonishing himself, Blore discovered that he was up for this. McCallum was taking the line of least resistance, and he didn't blame her for that. Indeed, he'd expected it. But he wasn't going to give her any satisfaction in the matter and was damned if he'd quit her office without putting across his point of view.

"They've closed ranks, haven't they?" he said. "Because there *is* something."

McCallum didn't reply, simply sat there looking down her nose at him, a grubby, out-of-work little man with a bad conscience, not long off the juice and probably missing it.

He turned to Whitlow, angry that he hadn't uttered a word since they'd got there.

"Come on, Chas. Aren't you with me on this?"

Whitlow stirred reluctantly, and the inspector turned her attention to him. She seemed a little apprehensive.

"Jerry's right. In the last couple of days something's cropped up, a new line of inquiry."

"And might I ask -?"

"You might." Blore jumped in, still seething. "A man called Chip Harper, a musician. It seems likely that he knew Anita Mead. He was the guy watching the guest house at Mardon. I'd say there's a distinct possibility he killed her."

"Jerry, Jerry." Whitlow was leaning across and tugging at his sleeve. "Slow down, chum. This is all speculation."

"At this point."

"Okay, at this point." Whitlow turned to McCallum, his tone respectful. "This is worth following up, Inspector. At the time I was investigating the Mardon angle, Tom Arnison pulled me off it before I could ID the watcher. He believed Mead's suicide closed the case and, well, I don't need to tell you about the top brass – they were pushing like crazy for a quick result. And because everything slotted so neatly into place, we didn't feel we needed to look further."

"And where do *you* think this is leading, Chas? Is Mr Blore simply allowing himself to get carried away?"

Whitlow shook his head stoically. At that moment Blore could have kissed him. "It's worth looking into.

Which we're happy to do, unless of course you feel you ought to take it over?"

It was a dig, and McCallum's eyes flashed, although she kept her voice level. "I've two murders of my own to investigate, ex-Detective Sergeant Whitlow, It might surprise you to know that they happened right at the end of this century rather than somewhere in the middle of it. Added to which, they've yet to be solved."

Touché. It was a slap-down for Blore too, although he felt that between them he and Chas had made the point. But the inspector wasn't finished.

"One more complaint like today's and I'm pulling the plug on this. Do you read me, Mr Blore? I can't let this sort of thing continue. These people have a right to get on with their lives. And Chas, if anything looks like happening from this 'new line of inquiry', keep me informed. You may be retired from the force, but I promise you I'll give you hell if you let me down."

Chas resembled a constipated effigy now. "Ma'am." The word, and the respect it was seen to carry, cost him everything. Anyone of a nervous disposition wouldn't have wanted to witness what was going through his mind at that moment.

"And then she can take all the flipping credit just for sitting on her fanny and doing bog-all," he grumbled, as he and Blore walked out of the building.

They crossed the road and headed down Speedwell Street to where Blore had left the car. A reception committee awaited them there, and he guessed it hadn't taken them long to find it. There couldn't be many battered blue Maestros around, eight years after they'd been discontinued.

Bobby Duggan was first to spot them and came storming up.

"We've had enough – *enough,* d'you hear? Hassling my mum, and now she tells me you've had the *nerve* to go back and see her today. I'm warning the pair of you. Keep away."

This tirade was peppered with epithets, but neither man reacted. Whitlow kept his head down and strode for the car. Blore, fazed by Bobby's wild eyes, simply tagged along behind, fingers clutching the car key in his pocket.

The Royces blocked their way, forcing them to a halt. Blore was immediately shocked at the sight of Nicky. 'Not a well man' was a serious understatement. He wore a heavy overcoat and seemed to bend under its weight, his face emaciated and drawn, his expression grim. He looked to be trembling slightly, and Blore guessed he didn't relish the confrontation, which wouldn't have been his idea in the first place.

Lorraine took a step forward. She didn't have any misgivings for sure, towering over her husband, lean and steely in leather jacket and tight-fitting jeans.

"Bobby, that's enough." Duggan had been ranting on, but her clipped command quietened him. "Inspector McCallum's spoken to them – they know the score." She turned a piercing gaze on Blore and Whitlow. "Bobby's got a point, even though he's not putting it across too diplomatically. They don't need all this dragged up again. They have treasured memories of a husband and father.

Can't you leave them be?" She glanced round at her husband. "And as you can see, Nicky's not in the best of health. *Please,* can I ask you once and for all just to leave us alone?"

She was looking at Blore, but it was Whitlow who answered. He spoke in the same respectful tone he'd used with McCallum, but again Blore suspected it wasn't what he was feeling inside.

"We take on board everything you say, Mrs Royce. But we've discovered a new slant on this, one that wasn't fully investigated before. Have any of you heard of a man called Chip Harper?"

Bobby, who'd been fidgeting all the while, now exploded with bitter laughter. "Oh, come on, granddad, you've got to be making this up! Who the hell's Chip Harper?"

Whitlow grinned, his eyes bright with mockery. "He happened to be a member of a little-known group called the Strawberry Eclairs, back in 1972. At the same time as your dad. Sonny."

It was too much for Bobby. With a strangled yelp, he went for Whitlow, hurling him back against Blore's car. For a few seconds the two men grappled with one another, until Blore and Lorraine rushed forward and pulled Duggan away.

Blore's first concern was for Chas, because he knew he had a heart condition. But the ex-DS didn't seem greatly troubled. He winked back at Blore, who was surprised by the lively, gloating expression on his face. He seemed satisfied with his handiwork, and Blore wondered if he felt their new lead was going to pay dividends.

Bobby was swearing fit to burst, not holding back at all despite Lorraine Royce's protests. He jabbed a menacing finger at Whitlow. "I'll have you, you old bastard. Just see if I won't. I'll *have* you!" Then he turned and stormed off.

The Royces fixed their attention on Blore, and he felt awkward. "I'm really sorry about this," he began.

Nicky waved the apology aside and spoke for the first time. "Mr Blore, we appreciate where you're coming from. But please bear in mind that all this happened nearly thirty years ago. As for Chip Harper, I knew him vaguely, but he wasn't ever part of our circle. Neither Phil nor I got into the drug scene, and as I recall Harper was right in the middle of it. We had enough problems dealing with Boyd's excesses and keeping him in line as far as possible. Where the Strawberry Eclairs were concerned, Phil was with them for maybe six months. He had a family to support and needed the income. But he didn't like the company and soon got out.

"So, Mr Blore, by all means chase up your new lead. Set your mind at rest, exorcise your demons. But how many times does it have to be said? It's been proved beyond reasonable doubt that Anita killed Boyd Neelan. The matter should be laid to rest."

Blore couldn't be sure whether or not Royce was playing to the gallery here, but as a plea it won hands down over Bobby Duggan's approach. Nicky had been courteous, and Blore felt constrained to reply in similar vein.

"If this leads nowhere, Mr Royce, I'll drop it. That's a promise."

"Thank you." It won him an approving nod from Royce and a tight smile from Lorraine. They said goodbye and walked off across the car park, Lorraine's arm through Nicky's, and he in need of her support.

As Blore watched them go, he was alert to Whitlow moving up to stand alongside him. He nodded at Blore, his lips compressed in a triumphant smirk. "So what do they know? As if you're likely to drop it now, eh, chum? Because it's going somewhere, and I reckon one of them knows it. Maybe more than one."

★★★

Blore wasn't a cheerful soul, not these days. When Cassie had come along, those first years when most of their time had been spent together, when life had been *good,* he remembered cheerfulness from then. This was probably as close as he'd got to it since.

Yet it wasn't cheerful so much as justified. Something was starting to happen: he was rattling cages – he, mean, grubby, washed-up little Jerry Blore – and people didn't like that. For him it promised a kind of hope, an indication that his gut feeling had been right, that his whingeing conscience could be salved: because Anita hadn't killed Neelan.

He hoped Harper was guilty and that they could prove it, because Harper couldn't be touched now and it was unlikely to matter to anyone. When he got home that evening, Ned Hargreaves had made good his promise to send him Harper's photograph.

He was pictured on stage, arm windmilling round to smite his guitar, huge gums bared in a yell, moustache spilling down his face, hair bushing out majestically as he stomped the boards in gold lamé platforms and red sequinned tunic and strides. Above all, in pride of place at his throat, hung that trademark green neckerchief. The photograph might prove useful in jogging memories.

Hargreaves phoned later that evening, and Blore thanked him. "Oh, think nothing of it, my friend."

Blore didn't, guessing that the lunch he'd coughed up for the other day had more than compensated.

"As it happens, I've been digging a little deeper," Ned went on. "And having quite a lot of fun. Our friend Chip was a busy boy. My sources link him with that much-loved actress Miss Suzy Steller. It may not mean a thing, of course." Hargreaves' gleeful tone suggested otherwise. "She was friendly with a great many people, notably the trouser-wearing sort. I've also discovered that she was a patron of Sacha's. Several back numbers of *Party Popsters* – now long defunct, I fear – contain a clutch of enlightening images. I'll send some photocopies: I'm sure the quality will be good enough to enable you to draw your own conclusions. Give me a tinkle when you've had time to peruse them."

Blore wondered if this was going to cost another lunch. He hoped not, but Ned was certainly coming up trumps. He expressed his gratitude again, and Hargreaves chuckled maliciously.

"Oh, there's nothing I like more than digging, Jerry my friend. It can bring such rewards. And as I said before, if your inquiries bear fruit, you'll be sure to remember your humble servant?"

Blore almost gagged on the 'humble' but promised he wouldn't forget. Once he'd got Ned off the line, he phoned Whitlow, related what he'd learned and outlined his intention of revisiting Ethel Robey and Suzy Steller the following day, armed with Harper's mug-shot.

Chas sounded weary. "Count me out, Jerry. The hospital have recalled me, so we'd better touch base tomorrow night. You're on your own, I'm afraid. Take care."

10

Blore didn't get the start he wanted next day. He zipped down to Mardon Regis full of hope and descended upon Seabirds eagerly brandishing Chip Harper's photograph. Albert met him at the door and informed him that Ethel was in a grumpy mood: her sciatica was playing her up.

She remembered Blore from the other day, repelled his opening platitudes by replying testily that she knew why he was calling and proceeded to examine the photograph through a magnifying glass.

Blore's hopes rose and fell several times before she handed it back. She told him she couldn't be sure. "They all looked alike, I'm afraid. This may well be the man, indeed it's more or less as I remember him – and there's nothing wrong with my memory. But I really can't say for definite. Maybe, and maybe not."

Blore thanked her and, somewhat chastened, made his way up to London.

When he'd phoned the previous evening, the lugubrious Waters had given him the name of the swanky hotel where her mistress was staying during the play's run. It had taken twenty minutes of patient probing to get this, the servant burbling on about not wanting to betray a confidence, and she guessed 'mum' would prefer it not to be known, as she probably wasn't staying alone.. Blore had the impression she could have given him the address straight off, without all the cloak-and-dagger stuff. But Waters sounded as if she'd been making free with the sherry if not the biscuits too, and he was simply glad to obtain the information and end the call.

He phoned the theatre and left a message to say he'd call at the hotel about midday, and to ring his mobile if it wasn't convenient. By the time he'd parked on the outskirts and taken the tube into the West End she still hadn't called, so he presumed she'd be up to seeing him.

The hotel was everything he'd expected: a commissionaire on the door and uniformed staff buzzing around a reception area big enough to accommodate a moderate infill of houses. Blore had dressed casually – never any other way these days – and with his customary *faux*-designer appearance had thought he might blend in with the clientele, but it didn't stop the clerk from looking like he had a bad smell under his nose. He brightened up at the magical name of Steller, but in the next instant became suspicious. "You're not a journalist, I hope?"

Why did these people pretend to dread journalists when all they lived for was publicity?

"I'm not. And I'm sure she'll see me." He wasn't, but at least he knew she was there.

The clerk rang through to Steller's room and, after a brief consultation, turned back to Blore. "Miss Steller will see you if you care to go up. Room 304. It's on the fourth floor."

Blore thanked him and went over to the lift, where he was catapulted upwards in the company of two other hopefuls similarly decked out in stubble and loose-fitting clothes. Judging by their aftershave, though, they also smelt of money, which knocked any further comparison for six.

As he made his way along the corridor, a door opened and a man came out. He looked to be in his late twenties, dressed in a baggy beige suit, white singlet and a couple of days' gingery growth. As they passed he threw Blore a tight smile, and Blore, nodding back, recognised Barry Grayston, Steller's leading man in the play and, if rumours were to be believed, other matters too.

Grayston had disappeared into the lift by the time he tapped on the door of 304.

"Enter!"

He went in to be confronted by Steller, lounging voluptuously on a *chaise-longue* and wearing a flowing garment of orange silk which covered everything and nothing at the same time. Blore knew she was a couple of years older than him, but she'd kept herself in good shape, even if that was partly thanks to a nose-job, boob-job and everything else-job.

"Jerry – darling!" Suzy unfurled herself from the *chaise-longue* and melted into his bewildered arms as if they were long-lost lovers. She bestowed a chaste peck on his cheek. "My dear, I won't ask what brings you here, but please, *please* don't tell me you made passionate love to Waters simply to learn where I was staying. A phone call to the theatre would have saved you the trauma."

She released him and gestured grandly to a top-heavy silver drinks trolley. He'd caught the whiff of gin on her breath and was repulsed by it, images of hotel bars at retail conferences and seminars flitting across his mind. The company drink culture, which had taken hold through the '80s and '90s, decreeing that if you wanted to get on in management you had to be ready and willing to prop up a bar into the small hours: true ability never came into it. And mindful of his career, he'd played along. Which was where it had all started to go wrong.

"Would you like –? Oh, but of course you don't, do you? Very wise. It's not only mother's ruin, I can tell you. Anyway, Jerry dear, come sit and tell me what it is you want to know. I – er, presume you're still a man with a mission?"

He confirmed that he was and allowed her to lead him by the hand to the *chaise-longue*, where she parked herself uncomfortably close to him. He felt he could put up with that as long as she didn't breathe in his face again.

"I have a name for you, Miss Steller."

"Lots of people have a name for me, Jerry. And darling, *please* don't be so formal. Call me Suzy. Oh, how I *hate* formalities."

He'd sussed that. "Suzy."

"And the name?"

"Chip Harper."

He'd hoped for a reaction. All he got was a shrug of her silky shoulders, but at least she let go his hand. "My, you've certainly done some digging. Not an archaeologist, are you?"

"Just a seeker after justice."

Suzy's response was a noise between a cough and a laugh. She got up, flounced over to the trolley and poured herself another gin and tonic, while flicking a cursory glance at the rest of the contents.

"Hhmmm, sorry. Nothing without alcohol. Sad reflection on me, I'm afraid. Can I get you a coffee or something sent up? Lemonade, water, ginger beer?"

"No, I'm okay, thanks. Chip Harper. Ring any bells?"

"Oh, a few. But very, very distant. I'm intrigued to know how the poor, spaced-out old sweetheart fits into Boydie's murder scenario. Perhaps you'd be so kind?"

He told her. As she listened, she rearranged herself on the *chaise-longue*, not as cloyingly as before, but still ensuring he could savour a flash of thigh and breast; as if he was likely to be tempted. Speaking, Blore kept his gaze on her face, alert for some reaction. He was disappointed to find none.

Once he'd stuttered to a halt, Suzy necked back the remains of her G & T and frowned at the ceiling. "Let's think now, Jerry. We're talking 1971, yes? Hhmmm, wonder how many guys in dear old GB looked and dressed like that? Cast of thousands, I'd say. And even your old sweetie-pie of a landlady couldn't be sure, could she?"

"That's a fair point. But what about the green neckerchief? That was a bit of a trademark where Harper was concerned. He's wearing it in the photo."

He brandished the photograph Ned had sent him, but Steller waved it aside. She set down her glass and stared at him levelly. Then her mouth twitched in a smile and finally she threw back her head and laughed. A musical trill didn't come near it. She cackled unashamedly, betraying her working-class roots, a mouthful of gold fillings and shed-loads of harboured bitterness.

"Oh heavens above, I see it all now and know I'm not wrong. Darling, don't tell me little Neddy's got his claws into you? He could be an absolute treasure if he wasn't such a bitter and twisted old thing. I've lost count of the number of times he's tried to get me into bed over the years, but it's equal to the number of times he's failed."

"But in any case," Blore resumed doggedly, as Suzy's laughter finally subsided. "Harper has to be a likely candidate. You knew him, as did Phil, Duggan and Anita."

"Oh, Boyd knew him too," Suzy countered easily. "Just that he wasn't in our immediate circle of friends. I mean, who'd have wanted him? He was a wannabe without much talent, and he grew more violent and resentful as it dawned upon him that he wasn't going to make it. But Jerry my love, the poor man's been dead for *yonks*. Yeah, sure, he was around. I may even have slept with him – he made enough unsubtle overtures – but it would have to have been one of those wild, wild parties when I was floating off into space and immune to everything.

"If I did – and I really don't remember – it would have been solely for the purpose of getting back at Boyd. I mean, that man put it about *everywhere*. He was insatiable. If it wasn't your Anita, it was some other wide-eyed not-so-innocent. He took the scattergun approach: laid anything willing and under thirty. He even went after Ginny Duggan and Stevie Royce: and two women more devoted to their men you couldn't wish to meet. He'd shrug it off whenever he was turned down. There were plenty of others who'd roll over for him."

"Let's get back to Chip Harper."

Suzy stifled a yawn. "If we must."

"He was jealous of Boyd. Might he not have reckoned he'd have a chance with you if Boyd was out of the way?"

"Oh, undoubtedly."

Blore believed he wasn't quite as gullible as he'd been a few days previously. But his heart began to pitter-patter at Suzy's casual reply, and he felt he might be on the verge of learning something worthwhile. Even though his reason warned him that his hope might prove false.

"But always assuming there'd been anything between us in the first place, it would have been ancient history by the time Boyd died." She smiled wryly. "I imagine vicious little Ned's given you the impression of Chip and I having a steamy affair, but I assure you that wasn't the case. To be truthful, I found Chip Harper rather scary, particularly if he was drunk or high – in other words, most of the time. No, he eventually got it together with a friend of mine, Claire Courtney. She's always been less choosy than me.

"Remember that I was with Boyd minutes before he died. Chip Harper was in London. I think he was with Hairpin Bend at the time, and he'd had a gig the previous evening. I'm sure darling Neddy can exhume a review of the concert. And by the by, I wonder who gave *him* an alibi for the time in question? You can't imagine anyone actually *sleeping* with him, can you?

"Anyway, back to Chip. The morning after the murder, I should hazard a guess that he was tucked up in bed with Claire at her pad somewhere in London. Saturday had been her birthday, and that night she'd thrown a seriously wild party. Sadly I missed it, as Boyd had got himself inconveniently murdered earlier in the day."

"And this Claire – after all this time, do you think she'd be able to give Harper an alibi?"

"I dare say. We still keep in touch. You can ring her now, if you like, because I've got her mobile number around here somewhere. And yes, I've no doubt she'll be able to remember that far back. Parts of us may be wearing out, but there's nothing wrong with our memories."

And there it was: Harper would have had an alibi. In the space of a few seconds she'd effectively pulled the rug from under his feet. He was floored and knew he was staring defeat in the face.

His dejection must have been obvious. Suzy seemed to recognise it and shunted a little closer to him, resting a beautifully manicured hand on his shoulder.

"You seem disappointed, Jerry. I'm sorry. In a way, I'd love Chip Harper to have been your man, particularly since he's long dead. Seriously, I don't think the police got it wrong the first time. But you won't give up, will you? I admire that. You really want to believe in her innocence."

He nodded, yes. He felt utterly deflated, because he'd been so sure about Harper. Or had he? Had he merely *wanted* to think that way and, in his desperation to point the finger at somebody other than Anita, ended up convincing himself?

Suzy was still busy with the pep-talk. "That's the real thing, y'know: belief. Listen, darling, I was once a skinny little eight year-old in a children's home. I've no idea how I came to be there. I remember my mother – just. I think she drank. As for my father, well, I've just blotted him out. He used to wallop her – both of us, probably, and that's how I ended up in care. *Care!* Huh! The staff were bigger bullies than my long-forgotten dad. But, Jerry, listen: I promised then that I'd make something of myself, and I did. Because I believed in *me.* And I had to fight every inch of the way, use my looks and body to become what I am now. *Fight,* Jerry. Pull yourself up and come back from this. You've done your best for Anita, but it's a cause that isn't worth fighting for any more. And if it's a friend you need, a shoulder to cry on, well, I'm here, baby. Here for you."

Her arm had snaked round his shoulders now, and she was brushing her super-inflated breasts against his chest, her free hand artfully caressing the inside of his thigh. "Jerry – darling. Who was the last person to do this?"

He couldn't answer. Because the last meaningful person had been Cassie: Cassie, whom he should have loved so much better; Cassie, whom he'd chased away.

And as Steller scrunched up closer to him, as he smelt once more the foul drink on her breath, he reacted in a way she could never have foreseen, lashing out at her with his free hand.

Ironically, it was nothing to do with the drink. That, oddly, even though he detested it, he could live with. It was the thought of Cassie, of he and she in one another's arms, of their love, their good times together; of those and all the other things he had so wantonly frittered away.

Suzy saw it coming late and ducked under the blow in the nick of time. Her evasive action liberated him, and he scrambled madly to his feet. "I'm sorry. Oh, dear God, I'm sorry -."

And for once in her life, Suzy Steller was speechless, sprawled back on the *chaise-longue,* showing off a mile of reasonable leg, her hair in her face and one huge, surgically-enhanced breast gaping through her silk garment. She watched aghast as he backed towards the door.

"I didn't mean -," he tried again. "I-I'm sorry."

She seemed incapable of replying, and as he came up against the door, he decided the best thing was to leave altogether. He squeezed out into the corridor, bustled along it and, not bothering to wait for the lift, fled down the stairs.

11

*H*e took her away from me. But I was certain it wouldn't last, certain that she'd come back. Drugs. Booze. That surely wasn't her scene. I'd known her well, and she just wouldn't have got into that sort of thing. His world and hers were poles apart.

So I waited, because I was sure she'd leave him soon. She would wake up one morning and realise he was worthless, that all men like him are worthless. And it would dawn upon her how much I'd loved her, and that she could depend on me.

And I waited, waited. But she never returned.

Ned Hargreaves must have caught the last post the previous day, because when Blore got home the promised photographs had arrived. They were photocopies and, as such, a bit grainy. Suzy in partying mode, clearly well away and draping herself over one man and then another. There was one shot, a poor one, of Suzy and Harper together, grinning inanely into the camera. But other people were in the frame too, all with arms round one another, so to say that the two of them were actually together was stretching it a bit.

In any case, Hargreaves' efforts meant nothing, merely underlining that he had no love and a great deal of antipathy for Steller, for whatever reason. Blore dropped the photos back into the envelope and pitched it on the table. He was unable to glean the merest shred of hope from them.

He hadn't felt this low for a long time, and that was saying something. He needed to talk to someone, wanted a shoulder to cry on, and the best he could think of was Whitlow. That was saying something too.

It was getting towards evening when he pulled up at Whitlow's bungalow, on the edge of a former council estate in Kidlington. The ex-DS answered his tentative knock, took one look at him and grinned, not unkindly.

"It's the brick wall, isn't it? Come on in, Jerry lad. I'll put the kettle on."

He led Blore down a long dimly-lit hall into a drab, sparsely-furnished lounge: carpet going on threadbare, a couple of ancient winged armchairs, TV, drinks cabinet, roll-top bureau, scratched coffee table with a wobbly leg. It didn't look as if Chas went big on entertaining or creating an impression, but who was he to throw stones?

Whitlow brewed tea, strong and sweet in large chipped mugs, and sat and listened while Blore talked through the events of the day.

"I can see why you're feeling down," he said, once he'd heard him out. "There's a chance that Suzy may have been bluffing, though."

He supposed Chas had a point but he was too preoccupied to think straight. The hopes he'd built up those last forty-eight hours had come crashing down, and he was wading sightlessly through their swirls of dust.

"The bottom line is that Chip Harper's out of the frame," he said. "And you were right: I was snatching at straws. The man watching Seabirds could have been anyone, as you said. It was a ruse cooked up by Anita to help her make her getaway."

Yes, a voice inside was nagging. *Make her getaway. So that she could get away from there and take her own life.*

And that didn't make sense. He knew that. But tiredness and confusion were overtaking him. He couldn't, didn't want to think.

"You were right too about the brick wall," he went on. "But I'm still convinced there's something not right about this. I don't know for the life of me what it is. But there's something someone's not telling."

"Listen." Whitlow clapped a sympathetic hand on the younger man's shoulder. "You've had a long day and a bad one. Let's draw a line under it, eh? I've not eaten, and I doubt if you have either. There's a decent pub a mile or so down the road, if you don't object. How about a bite? I'll pick up the tab."

Blore was grateful above all for the offer of companionship but admitted he was hungry too. "Nice idea. I'll drive, and I don't object to your having a glass or two. As long as you don't take it too hard if the conversation doesn't exactly sparkle."

Whitlow grinned. "Never reckoned you for a barrel of laughs, Jerry lad. But I dare say you'd put me in the same category."

"You're not far behind."

Chas laughed, and Blore, in spite of himself, lapsed into a smile.

The pub was a large one, busy for a weeknight, the food basic but good and plenty of it. They placed their orders, and Chas asked again if Blore didn't mind him drinking wine.

The nearness of the bottle, he supposed. There on the table, within such easy reach. He said it didn't bother him, knew there was no way he'd be even tempted to start necking it back. Only problem was, he wondered if he was starting to get hooked on mineral water. *The water of life.* He guessed it was the better option.

He found himself pondering, as Chas studied the wine list, the way he'd lashed out at Suzy Steller. Because she'd come on to him, and he could smell gin on her breath, and he'd hated the thought of her mouth closing down on his?

So he'd hit out. Just like – oh, dear Christ, yes, just like that time before. That time when it *had* bothered him. That time he'd staggered home drunk. *Drunk?* Try absolutely off-your-face kind of *battered.* Miracle upon miracles: that he'd managed actually to stagger when he'd been utterly legless.

Two years last July. Two years and three months ago. The blow, Cassie's scream, her tears. Yes, it had been the final blow.

"Cass – I-I'm sorry. I didn't mean to -."

"Jerry, you need help. You're sick. Look at you, you can hardly stand. And what's more, you can find it yourself. You've just made up my mind for me. I'm not sticking around for you any longer."

"I'll get help, I promise. Oh, Cass, whatever you do, don't leave me. I didn't mean to hurt you."

"Damn you, Jerry Blore. You've been hurting me for years. Years. Don't tell me you've only just realised it?"

"Give me one more chance, Cassie. Please – please, I beg you, just one."

But she wouldn't give him that chance. She'd suffered enough: the lonely evening hours, the bad moods, the drunken infidelities which he always denied despite the stench of some cheap perfume rampant on his rumpled suit.

By the next evening she'd gone, left while he'd been at work. No note, but years of warning. The day after that he went for counselling. In time for him, but too late for them. He hadn't seen her since.

"Penny for 'em, son?"

He wondered how long Whitlow had been watching him and guessing at what was going through his mind. He looked up, jarred out of his preoccupation. "Just thinking."

Not unnaturally, Chas misunderstood. "I'd say you'd given it your best shot – done her proud. And okay, you'll always believe you could have done more. But I reckon it's time to let go now."

"I didn't mean Anita."

"Who, then?"

"Cassie. She was my wife. I betrayed her – let her down badly."

"With the booze?"

"Not only that." *That last time he hadn't even known her name – wasn't even sure that he'd asked it. Two drunken hearts on bar stools, pouring out their woes. Shoulders to cry on. Why couldn't he have cried on the shoulder that mattered?* "Once I finally got back on track, I found there was a gigantic hole in my life."

"She left you?"

"Over two years ago now. Brought me to my senses, finally persuaded me to get help. I've lost touch with her. No forwarding address, and she's changed her mobile number."

"Tried her friends?"

"One or two. But if they know, they're not saying."

"Another three months and we'll be into the Millenium," Chas said. "I guess it'll be an emotional time. Maybe – well, people'll be getting in touch with each other."

It was kindly meant and brought Blore a spark of hope, quickly extinguished. Just that one chance had been all he'd wanted: to tell her how much he loved her, and that from here on in she could depend on him.

He grimaced. "That'd be too good to be true. Save it for some blockbuster weepie – I can't see it happening. No, I suppose that's been the point of the Anita thing: to try to fill that hole with something meaningful. I knew her well, Chas. We'd come through school together, friends as well as lovers. Annie could be a bit wacky, but she was a gentle soul. The more I think about it, the more I'm convinced she didn't do it."

"Who knows, chum? You could be right. But we haven't been able to talk to everyone, 'cos some aren't around any more. We're only ever going to get an incomplete picture. Hey, listen. Come the Millenium, how about you and me raising a glass together – something suitable for you, I know? To hope – eh? – wherever it might be. 'Cos I think neither of us is likely to be partying."

They were into their meals now, and Chas well into the wine. Something in his manner, a hint of regret, of pain, prompted Blore to ask the question.

"Your wife leave you too?"

Whitlow grunted. "Never got as far as the altar, lad. No, lovely girl, everything rosy. Then, before we were due to tie the knot, she thought about it long and hard and decided she couldn't put up with being a copper's missis. More likely she looked into a crystal ball and saw what a grumpy old sod I'd turn into a year or two down the line." He nodded at the bottle. "I took it badly, started down the slippery slope. Tom Arnison saved me, which was part of the reason I loved that man. He was a hard taskmaster, but a man of deep compassion. He'd been there too, you see. Talk about a policeman's lot not being a happy one. Years before, his missis had given him an ultimatum: her or the job. He chose the job. She took to booze and lit off with another man. Their kiddie ended up being adopted or some such, turned against Tom by the mother.

"Tom might not have been able to save his marriage, but he saved me. I owe him more than I can repay. I won't pretend there isn't something missing from my life. But once you've been down there, you don't ever want to fall that far again."

"No, I'm with you there. But I can't stop wondering about what I've lost. Everything I've thrown away and can't get back again."

Whitlow had refused coffee and was on the last of the wine. He was in a reflective mood, for when he spoke he seemed to be looking past Blore, far down the avenue of the years.

"Thrown away, snatched away. We're straws in the wind, Jerry lad. Blown here, there and everywhere."

"But don't you feel that somewhere along the way there has to be respite? Some sort of stability, a chance to lick your wounds, take stock and start again?"

"Don't you mean you wish? Well, maybe there is. I think I'm still waiting, and I'd guess you are too. Wondering if we'll ever get that chance again and, when it comes along, will we seize the moment? Jesus, how much more morbid are we going to get? Good job she's taken the cutlery away, or I'd be slashing my wrists. C'mon, Jerry, time to call it a night."

"Okay, let's be getting back. And thanks."

"What for?"

"For picking me up and dusting me down after I'd hit that brick wall. For trying to give me hope."

Chas threw a wry grin as he signalled for the bill. "If you find some, throw a little my way."

But he was in good spirits on the way home. He'd polished off a whole bottle of wine and was feeling buoyed by it. Disillusionment, as Blore knew only too well, would come with the morning.

In fact it came a lot sooner. Blore stopped the car and Whitlow got out, said goodnight and walked a trifle unsteadily up the path to his front door. Blore waited, expecting him to turn and wave once he'd inserted his key in the lock.

He didn't get the chance. The door suddenly opened, and Chas, who'd half-turned to deliver the anticipated wave, tumbled backwards over the threshold, legs flailing.

Blore gaped, wondering whether Chas had been drinking all day to have brought about such a collapse. Whatever had happened, it wasn't in the script, and he cut the engine, scrambled out of the car and hurried up the path to investigate.

He knew right away that Whitlow was okay, because he was swearing as if it had gone out of fashion and, although flat on his back, was tussling with someone who was trying to squeeze past him and escape from the house.

As Blore approached, a figure leapt nimbly through the doorway. It was dark, and all he glimpsed was a black leather jacket reflected in the street lamp's muted glow. The rest of his clothing was black too, leggings and balaclava. And he was light on his feet, alert to Blore's nearness.

The figure swerved to his left, and Blore flung himself at his legs, landing in a heap in the damp, overlong grass of Whitlow's apology for a lawn. He'd been pants at rugby thirty-five years previously and might have known nothing would have changed.

But the fugitive was still in sight, and Blore hauled himself up and gave chase. A winding path led deep into the estate, and he could hear light, sprinting footsteps which quickly grew fainter. A car started up, and he knew his pursuit was in vain. As he paused for breath, a set of tail-lights swung out on to the road and vanished into the distance.

But something had been left behind. Blore had sniffed it as the fugitive had burst past him. A trace of perfume, which, if pushed, he'd identify as Chanel No.5; although feminine perfumes had never been his strong suit.

Chas's front door stood wide open. Blore went inside and found the ex-DS riffling through the roll-top bureau in his lounge. He was still swearing volubly. He turned on hearing a footfall, his face a gnarled mask of anger. Seeing Blore, he continued searching. And swearing.

"Lost your life savings?" Blore asked.

Whitlow rammed the bureau shut and sank into a chair, finally beginning to calm down. "Picked the wrong house for that. There's nothing much I can't account for. No, there were some bonds – my old dad's. They've never once come up, not in forty years. But I don't want to lose 'em. Sentimental value and all that. They may not even have been nicked, probably I've put 'em somewhere else. It must have been some kid from the council estate, 'cos the back bedroom window's been jemmied, and I'd guess they came over the fence from the rec. Ruddy chancers – always giving me grief."

"If it's any use," Blore suggested, "it's likely your burglar's a woman. Very feminine perfume. I'd hazard a guess at Chanel."

"Flawed theory," Chas growled. "Could be a gay burglar or just some kid who'd nicked a load of perfume from his previous hit."

"Or not a kid at all," Blore added.

Chas nodded and held his gaze. The same thought was going through their minds. Chas's dad's bonds hadn't been taken. And the burglar hadn't been a coincidence.

But what had she (or he) hoped to find?

12

When he awoke the next morning, Blore felt a bit more positive about where he was heading. It stemmed from the aborted burglary, so Chas, if only in an indirect way, was responsible for this lifting of the spirits.

Blore thought he knew what the burglar had been looking for. Whitlow was an ex-copper revisiting an investigation, albeit in an unofficial capacity. It would be safe to assume he'd made some notes, maybe exhumed those he'd made at the time of the original inquiry. Might they contain something incriminating?

It was supposition, but lent him the impetus to continue plugging away at the Chip Harper angle. After all, there was only Suzy's word for it that Claire Courtney had been Harper's alibi. If he spoke to Courtney now, would Suzy have primed her? Perhaps Chas was right, and her invitation for him to phone her friend the previous day had simply been an outrageous bluff. He'd put nothing past Suzy Steller.

As he breakfasted, he eyed his mobile on the table beside him and decided he'd leave Whitlow out of the loop for the time being. The only person he hadn't approached concerning Harper had been Nicky Royce, and from what she'd said the other day, Lorraine would be in London. That was a bonus, for if she were present Blore was sure she'd try editing Nicky's replies. He'd got the impression at their first meeting that Nicky might have opened up if it had been just the two of them.

Just to be sure, he got down to Chelfold in good time and watched her leave. He parked the car a little way down the road and allowed a decent interval before calling at the house.

He had his apologies ready when Royce answered the door. Sorry to be a nuisance, but he was following up the new line of inquiry he'd mentioned the other day. No, it didn't mean going back over everything again. It concerned Chip Harper. Yes, he understood that Harper had never been part of their circle. But there were people who had known him, one of whom was Suzy Steller. Would Mr Royce mind if he…?

Nicky heard him out, then invited him inside, his manner distant but not unfriendly. He looked a haunted man, features paler, more pinched than previously. Huge bags under his eyes spoke of lack of sleep, and even at this hour – mid-morning – Blore could smell drink on him. Scotch, not the dreaded gin: but potent, deadly and offensive all the same. Still, he was confident he wouldn't react in the way he had with Suzy.

Blore was offered coffee, which he declined. Royce had something in a glass beside his chair. It had to be his first, with Lorraine having so recently left the house, but Nicky's generally dazed air suggested he might be mixing it with medication.

He offered Blore a seat and pitched down opposite him. "So, Mr Blore, tell me about this fresh line of inquiry."

Blore settled back in his chair and related what he'd learned about Chip Harper. As he'd said the other day, Nicky remembered him and confirmed most of the details already offered by Hargreaves and Ginny Duggan.

"I'd really like your opinion on this," Blore went on. "Might Suzy Steller have lied about Harper? Could she have used him as a hit man, possibly in return for sexual favours? She had no feelings for Anita and wouldn't have cared a jot about her taking the rap – particularly if she wasn't around any longer to speak up for herself."

Royce nodded wearily. "My friend, where Suzy Steller's concerned, anything's possible. And I'm biased, so not the best person to give an opinion. I never liked her then, and I don't now. Suzy was jealous of Boyd nabbing the limelight from day one of their so-called marriage. He had the greater claim to fame through his undoubted vocal talent. She only made her name by taking her clothes off and sleeping her way up the ladder."

This was grist to Blore's mill, and he switched smoothly to another tack. "It's been said you were the real talent behind the group's success?"

Nicky laughed, genuinely amused. *"Been said?* That sounds like Lori being loyal, bless her. No, it was never down to one person. We were a good team. Boyd was the extrovert, the front man who pulled the punters in. In that respect he left Phil and I in the shade, but that's where we were happy to remain. The pair of us were decent musicians – Ned Hargreaves recognised that. But we didn't have Boyd's drive, his get-up-and-go. He was the main man, and once he died, in the words of the song, the group had nowhere to go.

"I've never understood why we got on so well, Boyd and I, because we were poles apart. And he could have been greater still, up there with the immortals, but for the one weakness that proved his downfall. Women. They were there and available, and he couldn't leave them alone. Even when they weren't available."

Royce's tone had changed. There was something aggressive about it, which was at the same time disconsolate and forlorn. He emptied his glass, smacked it down on the table and got to his feet, stumbling, hand outstretched towards the portrait of Stephanie Royce.

Blore had observed on his last visit that it took pride of place. He thought now that it dominated the room, drew all eyes towards it and held them in thrall. He could understand Lorraine's barely disguised resentment of it.

Nicky turned back towards him. "He'd have taken her away from me, you know, whether we were best friends or not. Stevie had more talent, more grit, more nous in her little finger than Suzy Steller has in the whole of her much-travelled body. She doesn't bear comparison with my Stevie. Cheap and tawdry, that's all she was and is. And I'm sorry, Mr Blore, but I have to say it, your Anita was no more than a toy. I think she may have realised that, right at the end. It would have come as a shock, because Boyd would have charmed her, built her up, so that she thought she was on a pedestal."

Blore nodded, because he could understand that. Those young days they'd been together, Annie had had *nothing*. He recalled her face lighting up, her honest gratitude, on those occasions he'd bought her gifts. Cheap things, fripperies, but they'd meant so much to her. And yes, she'd been wacky, she'd been dizzy; and he could see how someone like Neelan would have had her in a total spin.

"He set Stevie on a pedestal too," Royce went on, his voice slurring, tears brimming in his haunted eyes. "You see, she was a woman who had *presence*. She could have been to him what she was to me. She *drove* me, motivated me, willed me to succeed. I couldn't have got by without her.

"She knew that, which is why she refused to play his game. She told me everything. There was no way she was going to leave me. But you see, Mr Blore, Anita wouldn't have seen it that way. Either way she was going to lose out. She thought he might take Stevie, and then Suzy came blasting in with her ultimatum. And that poor, witless girl's world came crashing down around her ears. Her only response was to turn round and give him *her* ultimatum. What did Boyd do? Laugh at her? Lash out? Swear? Ridicule her? We'll never know. All we know for certain – as plain as day, Mr Blore – is the outcome."

Blore took this in. Whether it was the drink or pills or both which had made Royce so forthright, he didn't know. What he knew was that he was nettled by the disparaging references to Anita. But they underlined the message he'd been given all along: that there was no further case to answer. Everything pointed to her, therefore she was guilty.

He hit back, no matter if it was below the belt. "She died, didn't she? Stevie?"

Royce's eyes narrowed. He'd been, for the moment, rocked by Blore's aggression: the scruffy, down-at-heel Blore, the unemployed, recovering alcoholic, the no-hoper. He turned away, his captive gaze ascending once more to his late wife's portrait.

"It was sixteen years ago that it happened. June '83: the twentieth anniversary of the birth of the Makeweights." He chuckled mirthlessly. "1963. Those really were the days. Phil Duggan and I met in a seedy bar in the East End. I'd written these songs and wanted to record them, put a band together. He was a drummer in search of a group, and I knew I could get hold of a decent bassist and somebody to play along on rhythm. So – could we make a go of it? It was about then I met Stevie: she convinced me we could. And hey, d'you know what, Mr Blore? I said to her I was thinking of getting these two new guys to make up a group. And she said, "Nick, you can pull *any* two guys off the street, and it doesn't matter how good they might be. You and Phil are the group: your songs and guitar, Phil's drums. Anybody else would just be makeweights." Then she grinned wickedly. "On second thoughts I'd say you were just makeweights too. It's Ginny and I who do all the organising."

"So that's where the name came from. Then, a year or so down the road, we met Hargreaves, he introduced us to Boyd and, there you go, the Makeweights became makeweights themselves. Ironic, huh?"

He was facing Blore again, the nostalgia making him smile, but its cruel irony causing him pain. Once more he looked back at her.

"It was Stevie's idea that we should celebrate the anniversary. No more Boyd, of course. Phil had moved on too. In fact, he was off the music scene altogether, writing his tutorials, teaching in workshops and schools. Me, I was performing solo, getting a good reception on account of the old days, but song-writing mainly. I didn't really want to do it, Phil neither, but Stevie reckoned it was a milestone worth celebrating. Beatles, Stones, Hollies: Boyd and the Makeweights weren't so far behind. I went along with it. I'd gone a bit flat, and she could see that, could see I needed pepping up.

"So there we were on a yacht in the Bay of Biscay: Suzy Steller, Stevie, me, Ginny, Phil and young Bobby. A number of others: friends, lovers and the like. Suzy had her latest squeeze with her: some racing driver who was all the rage in the mid-eighties – I can't even remember his name. And Ned with some starlet whose career he was about to launch: Sabrina Something-or-other. Anyway she was two feet taller than him and ended up laying several of the guests. Neddy wasn't among them, and, oh boy, he wasn't pleased."

Amusement was creeping in again, but as he re-focused on his story Royce pulled up short, his voice at once more serious and reflective.

"We all got sloshed. I mean truly, comprehensively battered. She – Stevie – went overboard. It must have been a complete accident. She just went up on deck and fell over the side. We all – or most of us – heard a splash and rushed up on deck. It was dark, and she'd, well, just *gone* and no-one had seen her. In fact, at first we didn't know it was her, and we had to sober up quickly and do a head count. But I knew, *knew* that it was Stevie. What I couldn't understand was why. Why did it have to be her?

"Y'know, I'd never in our whole – what? – twenty years together known her lose control. She lost it then, and I'll never understand why. I – I loved her so much. I didn't think I'd pull through: her death left such a void in my life. She'd been *everything* to me." He gestured towards the portrait. "Marshall – Adrian Marshall of the RA – painted it from a photograph. He captured her very essence. And I was low, Mr Blore, I sank so low. Eventually I was fortunate enough to meet Lorraine. She encouraged me to write, perform, live again. My goodness, she's been such a prop to me."

Blore was keen to drag him back to the matter in hand, because he could see a chink of light here. An idea – a possibility – was beginning to form. "Her body – Stevie's – it was recovered the next morning, wasn't it?"

"Eh?" For a moment, Royce looked stunned. "Oh yes – yes. We raised the alarm immediately, and it was practically light within the hour. The coastguard found her soon after. I – I identified the body. She seemed so peaceful. Poor Stevie. Not a day goes by without me thinking of her."

With that portrait staring down so imperiously, Blore wasn't greatly surprised. He fired his next question.

"Are you sure it was an accident? I mean, with everyone drunk or indisposed, might it not -? For instance, someone with a grudge?"

"Murdered?" Royce didn't sound too shocked. Blore thought he would have been almost enraged by the idea. Part of him, vicious in his disappointment, had hoped he would. "Well, let's put it this way. Nothing that could be proved. The police questioned us all closely. One of the guests – I think it might have been Suzy Steller – thought she heard a bump before Stevie hit the water. There was a contusion which suggested she might have struck her head on the side of the boat as she went in. It was generally supposed that she drowned.

"But no, there was no-one with an obvious grudge, and the coroner ruled it as accidental death. I've never thought it was anything other than a freak tragedy – one which I wish to God might have been avoided."

The front door swung open, and both men looked up with a start. Lorraine Royce stepped into the hallway, looking far from amused.

"Bloody buying meeting was cancelled, Nick," she called out. "At least I got the message in time to get off the train at Reading."

She was through the open doorway and into the room before she noticed Blore. For a moment she looked horrified and struggled for words.

"What -? Why are *you* here?"

Her gaze switched from him to the portrait to Royce. Blore began to burble an apology, but Nicky cut in front of him, placatory and suddenly in control, smoothly attempting to cast a veil over the booze mixed with medication and the idol worship of his dead first wife. Blore wondered if Lorraine was convinced.

"Angel, Mr Blore just dropped in for a chat. He's following up a lead about a man called Harper, a former musician. He mentioned him the other day. I've not been much help. I'm afraid. It's all okay."

She seemed to calm down then, removed her coat and offered to make coffee, a complete shift in mood. Blore wondered why she'd been so agitated at finding him there and supposed it was simply concern over her husband's health.

Blore said no to coffee and, after exchanging a few pleasantries, headed off.

He stopped for a pub lunch on the way back and ate it deep in thought. Once home, he took himself off for a long walk, a circular route round Witney, hardly meeting a soul. It helped him get his thoughts in order.

He liked the Steller/Harper theory. What if Suzy had killed Boyd, and Anita had either realised or even witnessed this? She'd picked up the knife and got blood on her hands. She'd panicked and fled to Mardon Regis. Suzy knew she had to be silenced, enlisted Harper, and he'd tracked Anita to Seabirds, stalked and killed her. End of witness, and the blame for Neelan's death left lying indisputably at Anita's door.

So what was Suzy's motive for doing away with Boyd Neelan? It wasn't Anita he wanted, but Stevie Royce. It was a real hunger, and Suzy couldn't bear being made to look a fool. Perhaps Boyd had boasted that he and Stevie were an item, their union a foregone conclusion? That would have had Suzy in a spin.

And leading on from there, twelve years later, in the Bay of Biscay: everyone, even the super-composed Stevie Royce, the worse for wear. What an ideal opportunity for Steller to take her revenge. The chance of a lifetime.

There was one thing more which no-one seemed to have picked up on at the time. Anita had left a clue. She'd booked into Seabirds under the name 'Susan Starr'. Close enough to 'Suzy Steller' to start someone thinking.

But no-one had thought. Arnison had pulled Chas Whitlow off the case before he could get started. *Why had that been?* A suspicion was forming in Blore's mind. An incredible suspicion.

Back to Suzy. He'd convinced himself that that was the way it must have happened. *Because no-one else had gone into the annexe between Suzy's departure and Anita's return.* If that was indeed the case, he had to admit that Suzy had deflected suspicion from herself very nicely. And possibly with a little help.

By the time Blore reached home, it was getting dark. The van must have been parked in the lane a little way up the road, awaiting his return. As he walked through the ever-open gateway towards the cottage, he heard the roar of an engine and squeal of brakes behind him. He turned as the van shuddered to a stop three feet away and was dashed to the ground by a figure which leapt from the driver's seat and felled him with a blow to the shoulder from a baseball bat.

13

It hadn't connected well, but he'd been caught off balance and went sprawling. He rolled over quickly so that at least he was looking up at his assailant, but fortunately the man had landed awkwardly in vaulting from the van and was struggling to stay upright.

He was dressed in black, a woolly hat covering the upper part of his face, but in the bright moonlight enough of his features were discernible for Blore to identify him.

Bobby Duggan.

His cheeks glistened with sweat, and there was a desperate twist to his mouth. As Blore seized the opportunity to scramble to his feet, Duggan took a pace forward, bat at the ready.

"This isn't the answer," Blore blurted out in a voice which sounded amazingly steady.

"Then get the message," Duggan cried. "You and that OAP copper. Just butt out and leave us all alone."

He swung the bat again but was too close. Blore saw it coming and blocked it with his arm. It was enough to make Bobby drop the bat, but before it hit the ground he swung his left at Blore, a haymaker, and the two men ended up in an uncomfortable, wriggling embrace.

One blast of Duggan's breath at close quarters told Blore that he'd been drinking. Indeed, had Bobby but known it, it came close to being a knockout blow by itself.

Sickened, Blore shoved the other man away, causing him to totter back and bang his head against the side of the van. Breathing heavily, Bobby came at him again. But Blore was ready: he saw the blow coming, ducked beneath it and jabbed his opponent on the jaw. Duggan went over but scrambled up again, just as a car drew through the gateway, its headlights illuminating his enraged face.

Game over. Bobby barged past Blore, dashing him to the gravel, clambered into the van and reversed out on to the road. He sped away, tyres screeching.

Blore sat there dazed, vaguely aware of a figure getting out of the car and running over to him.

"Jerry! What's happened? Are you all right?"

Lorraine Royce was bending over him, looking concerned. He must have seemed miles away, and in a sense he was, for even though he was still rocked by the assault, he'd just caught a whiff of her perfume. He could have sworn it was identical to that worn by Whitlow's burglar the previous evening. It couldn't have been conclusive, not with his questionable knowledge of perfumes. But might it have been Lorraine who'd broken into Chas's bungalow? And if so, why?

He put the matter on hold, replied that he was okay, apart from his shoulder which had stopped the baseball bat. She helped him to his feet.

"But who was it? Did you get a glimpse of him?"

He decided he'd better play it safe and shook his head. "Took me by surprise."

"There was a name on the side of the van," Lorraine went on. "But everything happened so quickly, I didn't have time to read it."

Just as well. Blore was pretty certain it would have been Duggan the other evening too: his tyre and Mum's pot. So what was it all about? Was it simply that Bobby was upset, that their questions had stirred up painful memories and he was being over-protective towards Ginny? Or was there something he knew about which needed to stay hidden?

Blore's head was spinning, not just as a result of his recent ordeal. Lorraine insisted that she should take him indoors. He didn't argue, just fished out his key, unlocked the door and ushered her inside.

"In all the excitement I forgot to ask," he said. "But what brings you here? Not that I'm not glad to see you: you couldn't have turned up at a better time."

"I simply came to apologise," she replied. "I was a bit sharp with you earlier in the day. It was only because I'm concerned about Nicky. His health's not good, and he's started hitting the bottle when I'm not around. I thought you'd come to hassle him, but he assured me that wasn't the case. Listen, you ought to let me take a look at that shoulder. Also, shouldn't you inform the police about what's just happened?"

"There's little point," Blore said. "I've nothing to give them, and if the assault bears any relation to my inquiries I know for a fact DI McCallum will say "I told you so." Not that I'd argue.

"As to the shoulder, I think it'll be okay. It was a glancing blow, and I guess it's only bruised. But now you're here, perhaps I can offer you a drink? I don't have any alcohol, of course. Just tea, coffee, water – the water's nicely chilled?"

She smiled. "Make it water, then. That seems to be what you're recommending."

He grinned back, went to the kitchen and took two bottles of Perrier from the fridge. He poured the water into glasses, added a slice of lemon to each and returned to the lounge.

She'd been taking stock of the surroundings: all relics from Mum's lifetime in the cottage, some handed down from his gran, some – most – that he could remember from his childhood. There was the ageing wallpaper with its swirls and twirls, the sofa whose creaking antiquity couldn't be masked by the fairly recent brown throw, the Welsh dresser with its rose-patterned crockery – probably Mum's wedding present – Gran's Spode plates and the scratched walnut sideboard bearing an empty porcelain fruit bowl and – the room's only trace of Blore – Anita's photograph in a makeshift frame.

He wondered what a woman who'd married money, as Lorraine had, would make of it and was sure she'd be too polite to say. He was also struck by her: for she was an attractive woman, trim and smart in a white body-warmer, tight blue jeans and tan calf-length boots. Her slightly sharp features and short but stylish blonde hair could make her look severe, but her face relaxed and mellowed when she smiled.

She was smiling now, perhaps in part amused by the room's bareness. But there was empathy too, for as she took the proffered glass she nodded towards Anita's photograph. He remembered it well: 1968 on Bournemouth beach, Annie in her swimming cossie. What a day out they'd had: his treat, and it had been as if he'd offered her the world on a plate. She looked radiant, stunning.

"This is her, isn't it? She was very pretty. You must have cared a lot for her."

He felt himself blushing, or as near to a blush as he could get on his stubbly, washed-out cheeks. "She was my first love. Things could have been so different. And how I wish – now – that they had. My mum – this was her house, bless her – didn't approve. Annie came from a broken home, had something of a reputation. But she was generous, gentle, kind-hearted."

He paused, for those adjectives applied to Cassie too. Another love, another betrayal. If he'd got his act together at those times in his life when he'd most needed to, might things have turned out differently? Annie and Cassie, his lost loves: lost, blown-away-forever opportunities for a sad man to have found himself a life. *Straws in the wind,* he seemed to remember Chas once saying. It came close.

Blore pointed Lorraine to a seat, the only one which didn't make a noise when sat upon. He parked himself across from her on the sofa. She seemed inclined to listen, so he talked. Not too much, because it would only have been about himself, and there was nothing in that forlorn subject of which he could be proud.

But the main thing was that she listened, and to an extent he was able to unburden himself: the career-obsessed drunk who'd chased away the wife who'd loved him and deserved to be loved in return. The divorce had gone through six months ago: he hadn't contested it. She'd simply had enough, had put up for too long with his self-inflicted working hours, his drinking hours, bad moods, longer and longer absences, petty, stupid little infidelities. Dear Christ, what hadn't she put up with? He didn't think there was another man on the scene. Maybe there was by now, and who could blame her? He'd hoped against hope that she'd return, but as day succeeded day he doubted she would.

"I'm sorry. I must be boring you to tears. But to sum up, I need to find a direction – something real and true. I'm floundering around in the dark, approaching fifty and with little or nothing to offer. I'm grateful to you for listening. I do apologise if -."

"Jerry." She held up a hand. "Jerry, you apologise too much. Thank you – for trusting me enough to tell me all you have. I understand why you're doing this for Anita. I didn't before, but I do now." She got to her feet. "I ought to go. Nicky will be fretting."

Blore stood too. "He relies on you a great deal, doesn't he? He said as much to me this morning."

Lorraine's smile made a brave face, but he glimpsed the anguish behind it. He could see why she came across as severe: she had to use it as a shield, otherwise she'd have been doubled over with the pain.

"He needs – I guess he's always needed – someone in his life to shore him up. That's what I've tried to do, but I don't come within ten miles of Stevie. She may not have been a paragon of virtue – he wouldn't perhaps have expected that. But she had tremendous will-power and strength of character, and they helped carry him along."

Lorraine took a step towards the door. Their hands reached for the latch simultaneously, and his closed over hers. It was unintentional and he panicked, wondering how she'd react, if she'd be offended. He was about to apologise when someone rang the doorbell, and they both leapt back startled.

He opened the door to find Whitlow standing there. It was hard to work out whose surprise was the greater. Lorraine gasped, while Chas's eyes opened wide. For once he was lost for words.

Despite his embarrassment, Blore was first to speak. "Er, Chas. Um – come in. You know Mrs Royce."

Whitlow recovered quickly. "I can call back if -?"

Lorraine snapped out of it but still looked flustered. "No, I have to be going. Nicky and I are due at a function in Reading this evening. He'll be wondering where I've got to."

"Thanks for calling," Blore stammered. He watched her to her car, waved before he closed the door.

Chas had installed himself on the sofa. He wore a mischievous grin and winked as Blore came back into the room. "Something you're not telling me, Jerry lad? I mean, she's not a bad looker, but a bit skinny and schoolmarmish for my liking."

"It wasn't like that," Blore began.

Whitlow waved it aside. "Nah. Pay no attention to me. Only winding you up. Seriously though – a social call?"

He knew he wasn't going to get off lightly. He offered Chas a coffee and fetched himself a second Perrier, not bothering with the glass this time: his concession to decadence.

"Hadn't heard from you all day," Whitlow went on, as he took hold of his mug. "So I reckoned I'd seek you out. Everything okay?"

Blore settled himself and gave Chas the lot: his visit to Royce, his latest Harper theory, the attack by Bobby Duggan and Lorraine showing up in the nick of time.

"Coming all that way just to apologise for being sniffy? Looks to me like she's got the hots for you, Jerry lad."

"If that was the case I could recommend a good optician," Blore countered. "But it's not. And anyway, Chas, what about you? All the way from sunny Kidlington just because you haven't heard from me today? I didn't know you cared."

Blore sensed at that moment that the mood had changed. Chas had been joshing him, and he'd been giving it back. But then the ex-DS had glanced down at the floor, the work of a moment, and Blore knew that he had something to say, something of portent which he wasn't going to like at all. When Whitlow faced him again, his expression had frosted over, his eyes hard.

Although when he spoke, his voice was slow and reasonable, and Blore could tell that Chas felt for him at that moment.

"Jerry, I think we should drop it now."

There was a long silence as Blore took this in. Throughout it, Whitlow continued to watch him steadily.

"You really want this, Chas? To drop it?"

"I reckon it's time," came the firm reply.

"But I think it's going somewhere. Don't you think that too? We've rattled cages. There's your burglary for a start -."

"Coincidence. As I said at the time, some chancer."

"What about Bobby Duggan? I feel sure we're getting close to something he doesn't want us to know."

"Or perhaps it's just his way of saying he's pissed off. We can't keep hassling these people, Jerry. They've answered our questions, and we've got to draw the line now."

Blore hesitated. He wondered about going back to the burglary. What if his gut instinct was right, and it had been Lorraine Royce? But he kept quiet, because he knew Chas wouldn't take it seriously: more pie in the sky. He tried another tack.

"Then what about Suzy and Chip Harper? My theory's possible, you have to admit."

"That it *could* have happened that way? Yes, lad, I suppose it could. But I don't buy it."

"You didn't investigate it either."

It was Whitlow's turn to be silent. He studied the floor again as seconds ticked by. When he looked up, his eyes were burning, and there was a small patch of colour high on his cheekbones.

"Now tell me just what the hell that's supposed to mean?"

But Blore held the upper hand and used the pause to allow Whitlow to seethe.

"Then give me a straight answer if you want me to drop it."

Whitlow's voice was taut and dangerous. "You're saying I've not been straight with you? Just where are you coming from, Blore?"

"Chas, *please*."

The ex-DS collected himself with an effort but continued to glare. "Fire ahead."

"Why wasn't the Harper angle properly investigated at the time? Chas, Anita signed in at Seabirds under the name 'Susan Starr'. Instead of just taking a pop at Suzy, couldn't it – shouldn't it have been – construed as full-bloodedly pointing the finger at her? Annie knew Suzy had killed Neelan. Suzy knew she knew and sent Harper after her. He followed her from Dreamfields to the station to Mardon Regis."

Blore had spoken with purpose, but he'd been aware from the moment he opened his mouth that Whitlow wasn't going to take this lying down. The colour had flooded into his cheeks, his fists were clenched, eyes starting out of his head.

"That's *shit!*" Whitlow gasped. "Why I'm letting myself get worked up I'll never know. 'Cos it's just another theory, isn't it, nothing earth-shattering or important? And like every single one of your prissy little theories, it sucks."

He sat for a moment gulping in air, willing himself to calm down.

He'd need to, Blore thought maliciously. *He didn't know what was coming next.* He didn't wish this on Chas, but he needed his reaction and, once he was capable of rational thought, his considered opinion. And okay, Chas was right, it was a theory. But he was beginning to believe it was somewhere along the right lines.

So he kept his cool, fought with the same intensity as the man seated opposite. "Tomorrow I'm going to ask Ned Hargreaves to do some more digging."

The mention of Hargreaves won him a malevolent glance, but Chas had his emotions under control by now. He shook his head sadly.

"Then you're wasting your time. I've told you till I'm blue in the face – you can't trust him. Can't you picture him now, sitting in his grubby little apartment, writing up every single one of your flaming theories and putting his spin on them so's he can sell 'em to the Sundays? He's just out for what he can get for himself. Give it up, Jerry. It's going nowhere. The truth is staring you in the face. Everything else is a lie."

"Fine, Chas. Then tell me why Tom Arnison pulled the plug on your inquiries in Mardon Regis? Why didn't he allow you to follow them up?"

"Jerry, I've already been through this -."

"Listen!" Blore was the one getting worked up now. "Is there a connection between Arnison and Suzy Steller ? Arnison's marriage broke down – you told me that. His wife took off, and their child was put in care. Suzy was a child from a broken marriage. She grew up in a care home. If she was Arnison's daughter, wouldn't he have wanted to protect her from a murder investigation? And again as you said, the top brass wanted a result. There was an obvious solution to hand – a ready-made excuse for him to put a stop to the investigation."

Whitlow was perfectly still. He'd calmed down almost to the point of inertia, his face now deathly pale.

He stared aghast at Blore, slowly shaking his head in disbelief. "Sweet Jesus Christ, you can't be serious. Tell me you're not. Or at least give me some indication that you've not completely lost the plot? Suzy Steller – Tom Arnison's kid? Oh lad, you're sick. What's up? Got a craving to get back on the juice, and it's turned your mind?"

"Now come on, Chas -."

"No!" Whitlow was yelling at him, starting forward out of his seat. *"You* come on! Because I'll tell you this, chum, for stick-on, sure-fire certain, we're not going down that road. If you are, then leave me out, okay? All you're doing – all you've ever been doing – is snatching at straws, and any straw will do."

"But I'm convinced -."

Chas was on his feet, seeming to tower over him, and Blore felt pinned to his seat as an accusing finger was jabbed in his face.

"Convinced, nothing! You're *hoping*, that's all. And tunnelling deeper and deeper into the past because you haven't got the guts to face the future. Oh, just get lost, lad. I'm out of here."

He barged his way to the door, yanked it open and slammed it shut with such angry force that the windows rattled. He slammed his car door too, gunned the engine and roared away into the night.

While Blore got slowly to his feet and stood, head bowed and disconsolate. Because he knew that what Chas had said was right.

He still clutched his bottle of water, found himself clinging to it, as if it was his last hold on life.

14

I 've given this weeks of thought: painful, grinding weeks. I'm not judging him lightly but I've reached the conclusion that he must pay for what he did. As if it wasn't bad enough, to have her snatched from me in that way. I suppose the years have helped cushion the blow, helped me learn to live with my rejection, go ahead and plough my own furrow. The drinking helped for a while: helped me forget.

But that's all behind me now. And the residue is bitterness. I know now and at last what I didn't know before. And I'm determined to make him pay.

★★★

Exhausted by the day, Blore soon gave up on television, turned in and fell asleep almost immediately, finally awakened by the insipid jangling of his phone. He was amazed to find that it was after 9 a.m., and that he'd slept for almost eleven hours.

That wasn't all that amazed him: the caller was Whitlow. Blore had been convinced he'd seen the last of him after their spat the previous night.

But Chas's tone was terse, and he didn't waste time on preliminaries.

"Get yourself along to Oxford nick. Our lady of the stiletto requests our presence."

"What time does she -?"

"Ten minutes ago. See you there."

He rang off to leave Blore pondering the reason for this latest summons. It couldn't be another ear-bashing: they'd surely not succeeded in annoying anyone else?

He was there within half-an-hour, sitting alongside a glum-looking Chas in reception. The two men had acknowledged one another with a nod, but neither spoke. And McCallum, as if anticipating their unease, made sure she kept them waiting, twenty minutes again, before ringing down to the desk to have them shown up.

The first glimpse Blore had of her made him think again about the ear-bashing. It also made him wonder if he had stomach for the fight. Because fight there promised to be. McCallum glowered at them and pointed to seats, which the two men took without a word.

"Gentlemen." The inspector's lips tightened in the antithesis of a smile. "Let me inform you that, while they were out last night, the Royces' house was burgled. I'm assuming that comes as news to you?"

Her tone was remarkably light, but she was watching them both like a hawk.

All she could have gleaned from Blore's witless expression was shock.

"Someone must have been looking for something," he murmured.

Whitlow shifted in his seat as he raised his eyes to the ceiling. "The boy's brilliant," he sighed.

Blore pulled himself together. "What was taken?" he asked.

McCallum shrugged. "Nothing as far as they can make out. A window was jemmied at the rear of the house some time between when they left at eight and arrived back at eleven-thirty. It was a professional enough job for the burglar to know how to silence the alarm."

"A window jemmied." He looked across at Whitlow. "The same thing happened to you the day before."

Whitlow's groan was audible, and McCallum jumped in immediately. "Got yourself burgled, Chas? Why wasn't it reported?"

The ex-DS bequeathed Blore an unfriendly glance before facing the inspector. "Because it was kids, ma'am. It's happening all the time on the estate, the usual mixture of bravado and boredom. With respect, they never seem to get caught."

"So what were they after? Your life savings?"

Blore couldn't guess what Whitlow's reply might have been, other than it would have carried some implied insult to the inspector. But it was his turn to jump in now, and feet first, because he feared they were getting away from the point.

"Evidence, of course." The other two turned indignantly, as if questioning his right to an opinion. "This is all tied in to the questions we've been asking. Someone's feeling the pressure and is starting to panic."

As he was speaking, Blore realised he had something to beat them over the head with: his strong suspicion that Whitlow's nocturnal visitor had been Lorraine Royce. And it was a bit rich, wasn't it? Lorraine doing a spot of burglary, then twenty-four hours later getting burgled herself?

He was determined to keep a lid on it for now, certainly until the time that he could furnish a motive for the burglary. He needed Chas's opinion but couldn't be sure if they were still on speaking terms. If not, he'd just have to go ahead, plough his own furrow.

He went on, sensing the plea in his voice. "Inspector, surely this has to encourage you to reopen the investigation?"

He was alert to Chas shaking his head cynically as McCallum, eyes flashing, skewered him with a glare. "With my caseload? A thirty year-old mystery that got itself dead and buried at the time? Do I *look* that stupid, Mr Blore?"

But Blore was fired up. He told McCallum about the Chip Harper angle and a possible link between him and Suzy Steller. He brought in Bobby Duggan's threats, taking care not to mention the assault the previous night.

To her credit, the inspector heard him out. Her head bowed, she sat tapping a pen on her notepad. Once Blore had finally ground to a breathless halt, she looked up and smiled viciously.

"And your proof?"

Chas was shaking his head again. "Jerry, you're going nowhere with this. Leave it be."

"But Chas, the burglar at your house – probably looking for your notes on the case."

"It was some kid. As I said before, it happens all the time. And I never made any notes."

"We know the burglar was a woman. I smelled perfume –?"

"So? Women are exempt? They do everything men do anyway, even if they don't do it half so well."

This was a nasty tilt at McCallum, but the inspector didn't give it the time of day. She was studying Blore, trying hard to appear sympathetic.

"Mr Blore, I'm sorry. But without any proof, everything you've said is no more than speculation. I simply can't build a case on what you've given me."

Blore could see she was drawing a line under it, and he'd had enough anyway. He stood up. "Thanks for your time, Inspector."

"Before you go – neither of you know anything about the Royces' break-in?"

Both men shook their heads, and Blore left the room. He heard the mumble of discussion between the other two, although he couldn't think what they might have to say to one another. However, Chas had caught him up by the time he got down to reception.

"Jerry – wait up."

He turned, expecting some valedictory barb from Whitlow. But the older man's face was serious and sad; and he looked desperately tired.

"Jerry, lad. I'm sorry."

Blore's lips twisted in a smile. "Me too. Thanks for all you've done, Chas."

The two men shook hands before heading off in their different directions.

★★★

By late afternoon Blore was back in Oxford, something he certainly hadn't expected.

He'd returned home that morning glad that he and Whitlow had healed the breach, but downcast that he appeared to have reached the end of the line. He still believed there was mileage in the Harper-Steller issue; and then the burglaries. Why had Lorraine Royce – assuming it had been she – broken into *Chas's* house? And why had the Royces themselves been burgled? He couldn't see at that precise moment how he might be able to supply answers to those questions. But he didn't have to wait long for something new to turn up.

He'd managed a bite to eat before the phone rang. It was Ned Hargreaves, sounding as if he'd just won the lottery.

"Jerry? I think I may have found an important lead, and I'm sure you'll want to be in on it. We need to meet."

Blore jumped at the chance. No way he'd put money on it, but he wondered if Ned's discovery might not answer one or two of his own burning questions. The rendezvous was Oxford, Christ Church Meadow at the St Aldate's end at four p.m. Hargreaves was just boarding a train at Paddington. Blore grinned as he clicked off the phone: they'd be meeting within a stone's throw of the nick. If McCallum saw him, she'd probably have him picked up for loitering.

Ned was waiting on a seat not far from the entrance to Christ Church. People were milling around, students and tourists for the most part, oh-so-wise amplified voices, staccato chatter and the blinding flash of expensive cameras. Ned sat alone, no-one paying him the least attention, despite the fact that he was resplendent in green suit, yellow T-shirt with 'Rock Lives!' emblazoned across it and snazzy white state-of-the-art trainers. His face shone with self-congratulation: the cat – or was it the toad? – who'd got all the cream.

"Hi, Jerry! Over here. Take a pew, my friend. I've brought you coffee. Enjoy!"

Blore thanked him and sat. He took a slug of his coffee out of politeness. It was *latte*, sickly sweet, and he had to work hard to turn his grimace into a somewhat cynical smile. "We've cause for celebration, then?"

"I should say we have – and that's being ultra-conservative. Jerry my friend, this is not only big, it's hot. It's Pete Ramsey, old chap. No less than he!"

If it was hot, it had a distinct advantage over the coffee. Blore wondered if he was being dense. "I'm sorry, but who's Pete Ramsey?"

Ned chuckled complacently, his grin stretching wider. "Oh, silly me. Of course, you wouldn't know. Jerry – my profuse apologies. But I guarantee the end result will be worth the confusion. Pete Ramsey is, or was, a musician; generally a session man. He played bass guitar for a number of bands throughout the seventies, the most notable being Hairpin Bend."

"Chip Harper's group."

Hargreaves nodded vigorously. "Spot on. Although he was with them for little more than two months. As I recall, Jimmy Maskell, their regular bass man, was in rehab and Pete filled in for him. One of those months was September 1971.

"When Boyd Neelan was killed." Blore was finding himself growing less cynical by the second. Even the coffee was slipping down unnoticed.

"Absolutely."

"But how did you manage to find him?"

Ned gave a cheesy grin. "Oh, my friend, *he* found *me*. Wheels within wheels, y'know. I put out feelers here and there, and information is fed back to me. There are few people better connected in the music business than my good self. Maybe none."

His conceit was beyond belief. Talk about a self-congratulatory pat on the back: this was a full-blown massage. On another day Blore might have felt like flattening him. Today he didn't care about anything other than getting the case back on the rails. His gut feeling told him this was leading somewhere. Although he recalled with discomfort Chas's stern warning: *there'll be something in it for him.*

Hargreaves was about to elaborate on how clever he'd been, when a man came shambling over to them. Blore had him down right away as one of Oxford's homeless: unkempt, shoulder-length hair streaked with grey, tatty black bomber jacket, ragged jeans and unspeakably filthy trainers.

Ned's smug expression somersaulted into one of revulsion. "Sorry, old pal. This seat's taken. We're expecting company any minute."

The man guffawed croakily. "Company's here. I'm Pete. You gotta be Neddy."

The expression went into fast rewind. "Pete? Oh, Pete, yeah, yeah, sure thing, cool. And I'm Ned, right? Ned Hargreaves. Good to meet you, Pete." Ned leapt from his seat, liberally sprinkling coffee over Blore. He offered a hand, which Ramsey ignored as he shoved past and sprawled on to the seat next to Blore, taking up the remainder of it and leaving Ned standing.

"Er, get you a coffee, Pete?"

"No, ta. Got this." Ramsey conjured a can of Special Brew from the folds of his jacket and took a generous swig. He switched Blore a shifty glance. "You all right, mate?"

"Jerry Blore. Hi."

"Yeah, right."

Ned was back to his most unctuous as he reclaimed Ramsey's attention. "Jerry's a pal of mine. He's looking into a murder case from some years back. Boyd Neelan, no less."

"Boyd." Ramsey smacked his lips. "Yeah, remember him well. A legend, a real legend. Played a couple of his gigs – only a lot farther down the bill."

They laughed, Ramsey looking from one to the other of them, not letting his gaze linger on Blore. He supposed that was because Pete saw Hargreaves as the main man, and he didn't mind that. He was sure Ned would be asked to part with some money, and for himself Blore wanted to see where this was leading. Pete didn't exactly come across as a reliable source of information.

But Ned seemed to think otherwise. "Right, Pete. Now you told me on the phone -?"

"About Chip Harper. Yeah, yeah, remember him too. But –er, before you go on, you said -?" He grinned wolfishly, rubbing his fingers and thumb together.

Ned got the drift. "I'll make it worth your while, Pete. A man of my word – Jerry'll tell you that. Let's hear what you've got to say. You played with Hairpin Bend, right? September and October '71?"

"Yeah, on bass. Jimmy Maskell went overboard on the shit – mind you, who didn't from time to time? I got drafted in as replacement, though Jim was back before Christmas. Decent band we were. Never got the breaks we deserved."

"And that's how you came to know Chip Harper?"

Ramsey chuckled throatily. "Oh, yeah. He was the kind of guy you never forget easily. A wild man, a real party animal. And man, was there some parties. Booze, dope, chicks, all laid on – or laid out. You never went away empty-handed."

"And Harper went along?"

"Shouldn't think he ever missed."

"So, Pete, for Jerry's benefit now. Who was Chip going around with at the time? He was seeing this chick, right?"

"He was always seeing some chick, man."

Blore sat and watched them. He felt like a detached observer and, whether or not he was prompted by the ever-doubting spirit of Whitlow, the idea slowly dawned upon him that something wasn't right. This was all too easy.

He studied Ned and didn't question the fact that the little man was in deadly earnest. Ned shuffled his feet restlessly, his ugly face glistened with sweat and expectation and his eyes were popping.

While Pete Ramsey was totally laid back, lolling on the seat as he swigged from his can. He kept running a hand through his long, greasy hair, hair which almost completely obscured his face.

"Yeah, pal. Now let's get to see the dosh before we go any further."

Ned fumbled for his wallet, fat with credit cards, almost dropping it in his excitement. He counted out five ten-pound notes. Ramsey snatched them, stuffed them inside his jacket and held out his hand for more.

"You said a hundred bars on the blower, man."

"In good time, Pete. First tell me what I need to know."

Blore was beginning to find Hargreaves' desperation comical. So he decided to prolong the agony: the spirit of Whitlow again.

"We heard Harper's girl was an actress called Claire Courtney," he put in, earning a glance of reproval from Ned. "She the one you remember?"

"Claire? Yeah, remember her. Yeah, she put it about like there was no tomorrow. Sure, Chip was seeing her some of the time. As I said, he was always nobbling some chick. But I don't think hers is the name our little roly-poly mate is busting a gut to hear." He threw Blore a mischievous grin, and for a brief moment he glimpsed Ramsey's eyes: lively and sparkling, not at all the eyes of a nearly down-and-out.

Ramsey turned back to Ned. "Hand over the rest of the dosh, pal. 'Cos as you've been pissing yourself to hear me say, the chick in question was Suzy Steller. Them parties I went to at the time, generally she was there, and everybody was out for a piece of her. More often than not Chip got lucky – or at least that was the way he told it."

Ned Hargreaves looked utterly drained as he parted with the remainder of the cash. But his eyes were alive with malicious glee.

"Pete, my friend, you're a star. Listen, here's my card. Give me a bell if you remember any more –er, tasty details. I can't tell you how big this is going to be. I'll probably need to touch base with you again before long. Where can I reach you?"

"25 Horton Avenue – just off the Abingdon road. You'll have to drop by, there's no phone. Oh, and it won't be for free, neither."

"You'll be well paid, never fear. Thanks again, Pete. I'll be in touch."

Ramsey finished his Special Brew with a flourish, belched and threw the can on the ground. He waved languidly at Blore without making eye contact and shambled off down the path, barging his way through the middle of a clutch of tourists.

Blore watched him go. And wondered.

15

In the meantime, Hargreaves was having difficulty containing himself. Glee was oozing from every pore of his ugly countenance, as he excitedly shuffled his smartly-shod feet in the Oxford dust.

"Jerry, my friend, we've cracked it. You've something to take to the police. With a living, breathing witness, they'll have no option but to take another look at the lovely Miss Steller. But please, allow me to beg one small favour. Wait until the end of next week. I shall miss this week's deadline but, as soon as I've written up this little lot, I shall be doing the rounds of the Sunday tabloids in search of the highest bidder."

"Listen, Ned, I can't be sure -."

Ned waved aside the protest and thrust out a pudgy hand, which Blore shook reluctantly. "Thanks for seeing it my way, Jerry. Must dash now. Off back to my pad *toute suite*. This, my friend, is going to be big, big, *big*. Of that I'm certain." He bared his teeth in a demonic smile, turned and scurried away.

Blore let him go. He scoured the distance for Pete Ramsey and glimpsed him on the far side of a rugby pitch where a group of muddy, tow-headed schoolboys were flinging themselves inexpertly around under the auspices of a track-suited, whistle-happy master. With a despairing glance at Hargreaves' departing figure, Blore made up his mind and hurried off in pursuit of Ramsey, suspicion increasing with every step.

Ramsey had told them he lived off the Abingdon road, so why was he heading in the opposite direction towards Magdalen Bridge? Perhaps there was a good reason, but there'd been something about Pete which, for Blore, hadn't quite rung true. Something, what – *familiar*? There'd been the incongruously lively gleam in his eyes, the way he'd tried to keep his face obscured from Blore's scrutiny, hiding behind that lank curtain of hair. *Why?*

So that Blore wouldn't recognise him?

By now he wasn't far behind. Ramsey was still slouching along, intent on playing the part. Blore kept in the shadow of the high wall as his quarry turned out of Christchurch Meadow into Rose Place.

The car was parked halfway down the cul-de-sac. A Mercedes in blushing pink: unmistakable. Pete Ramsey trotted up to it, swung open the passenger door and ducked inside. As he did so, he whisked off his long grey mop to reveal the grinning features of a much younger man with curly red hair and a stubbly face: Barry Grayston.

And if there'd been any doubt that Blore's sight deceived him in the fading light of late afternoon, there was no mistaking Suzy Steller's strident laughter as she eased the car to the end of the road and out into the Magdalen Bridge traffic. Blore checked his watch: they'd probably calculated a quick zip back up the M40 to reach their theatre in good time for the evening performance. How he hoped the grinding Oxford rush hour wouldn't scupper their plans!

He turned, intending to make his way purposefully back to St Aldate's, and collided full-on with a figure scuttling towards him.

An apology started from his lips; aborted the moment he caught sight of the green suit and screaming yellow T-shirt.

Ned Hargreaves was eyeing him suspiciously, but Blore, nettled by the realisation that Ned had been following him, jumped in first.

"I thought you were in such a hurry to get back to London?"

Ned's eyes narrowed. "I happened to observe you take off at a canter in the direction Pete had gone," he said tartly. "You weren't by any chance intending to cut me out?"

Blore noted the underlying menace in the little man's tone, but even that couldn't stop him laughing.

"Did I say something funny?" It was Ned who was nettled now.

Blore returned to looking serious. After all, it was no joke, simply a waste of everybody's time.

"Not at all," he replied. "I was following our Mr Ramsey because he'd aroused my suspicions."

"Suspicions? What d'you mean?"

"How well do you know him?"

"Know him?" Ned was beginning to sound like a shrill, nauseating little echo. "I don't, to be frank. But if you really don't believe me, go ahead and check for yourself. Pete Ramsey played with Hairpin Bend in September and October of '71."

"I'm not disputing that. But your only previous contact was when he phoned earlier today?"

"That's right."

Ned still looked affronted; a little hurt too, and Blore guessed that he was a vulnerable soul beneath the veneer of pride and self-importance. He thought he ought to try to let him down gently, but saw no way of doing so. *Oh well, the jugular it was, then.*

"Well, get this. The man you've been talking to isn't Pete Ramsey."

"Oh, my friend. You're being ridiculous. He phoned me -."

"I accept that he phoned you. But the phone call doesn't prove anything."

"But -?"

"He's *not* Pete Ramsey. Because he's better known as Barry Grayston, an up-and-coming young actor who just happens to be Suzy Steller's latest leading man. I just watched him get into a car in Rose Place. A pink Mercedes. Suzy was driving. I'm sorry, *my friend*. But it was all one big wind-up."

"Are you – sure?" What little colour there'd been had drained from Ned's face. Bundling past Blore in an unwonted burst of energy, he waddled to the gate and stared forlornly through the bars, as if by doing so he might persuade the pink Merc to make a magical reappearance.

Blore sauntered over to join him. "They drove off five minutes ago, and I promise I'm not kidding you. The whole Pete Ramsey thing was a hoax – and they've relieved you of a hundred bars into the bargain."

Blore was trying not to gloat and making a poor fist of it. But if he'd thought Hargreaves would be at all downcast, he'd have needed to think again.

Ned was furious. His eyes bulged, his usually pasty face was bright with anger and his soft fists were knotted. He spat words like bullets.

"I'll pay her back for this. Pay her back, d'you hear me? The conniving bitch, if she thinks I'm going to forget this in a hurry. I'll not be made to look a fool by her. She'll suffer for this, I promise you. She'll suffer…"

"Well, at least you won't be writing your article and risking a libel suit," Blore assured him lightly.

The glance he received in response was a long way short of friendly. Ned stomped off in the direction they'd come, his state-of-the-art trainers ruthlessly mashing the gravel. Blore was hard put to keep pace with him. But he didn't intend to let him slip away right at that moment.

"One more thing."

Ned looked at his watch. "I've a train to catch," he snarled. "And as you may have noticed, I'm not really in the mood."

"I'll make it quick." Blore's tone was peremptory, showed he wasn't messing, and he immediately sensed that the little man was on his guard.

"Well?"

"Boyd was intending to replace Phil Duggan?"

"Oh, that. It was mooted, yes. With Sonny Ralston. But what of it? It was no more than a whim. Boyd had them often. Rather a restless soul, dear Boyd, as you'll no doubt have gathered by now."

"Did he ever try to replace his manager?"

Ned skidded to a halt, gravel spurting in all directions. He was still angry, Blore had expected that. But he seemed to be increasingly on the defensive.

"Replace *me*?" His voice had lost its earlier tetchiness. "No, my friend, no. Dear Boyd would know better than to do that."

Blore shrugged, recognising the need to mollify the little man's outraged ego. "Daft idea, I know. But I had to ask the question all the same. I mean, he tried to replace one of the best drummers in the land…"

Hargreaves had resumed his fast waddle, with Blore loping along beside him.

"So you wondered if he might not try the same with one of the best managers?" Ego back on track, but Blore had observed something there for a moment: apprehension, perhaps, or maybe something more sinister? He recalled Ned's rage of a few minutes previously. He'd known from their first meeting that Hargreaves had claws: perhaps they were sharper than he'd imagined.

"Well, he might have kidded himself that he could have done without Phil, but not *me*. I *created* him, you know. And anyway, I'm sure the thought would never have entered his head. Ah, a taxi. I must be on my way. Good day, Mr Blore."

Ned bolted for St Aldate's and Blore let him go, making his way back to the car park in a more sedate and thoughtful manner.

Why, he wondered, did Ned so badly want to implicate Suzy Steller? Some old score to settle? Or might it be a way of deflecting suspicion because he himself had something to hide? That afternoon he'd struck a nerve, had had a glimpse of the real Hargreaves festering beneath the synthetic jolly-good-fellow exterior. He hadn't been surprised.

And of course, Ned hadn't been investigated at the time of Neelan's murder. It had been Chas who'd raised the question about the likelihood of Boyd wanting to replace his manager. Well, when next they spoke, Blore thought he just might ask Chas to take a closer look at

Ned Hargreaves. He didn't think the ex-DS would need a second invitation.

On the other hand, the Pete Ramsey scenario just played out could have been a daring double bluff on Suzy's part. What if Chas (again) had got it right and she'd really been involved with Chip Harper, dreaming up the Ramsey ruse to throw them off the scent?

Blore had no time for further reflection, because his phone went off at that moment. To his surprise it was Nicky Royce, his voice muffled and distant. He wanted a word with Blore about something he couldn't discuss over the phone. Royce asked if he'd pop over to Songrise, reckoned it'd be worth his while.

Blore explained that he was in Oxford and would get to Royce in half-an-hour, traffic permitting. Ideas, openings, new initiatives were coming at him thick and fast. He couldn't guess what Nicky might have for him but viewed it as a plus.

So it was that he fell foul of the rush hour he'd wished upon Suzy and Grayston. It took half-an-hour to crawl the two miles to the A34, and it was just before six p.m. when he pulled into the drive at Songrise. He arrived a few seconds behind Lorraine Royce, who was about to unlock her front door. She turned on hearing his car and met him with a puzzled frown.

"Jerry? What brings you here?"

He explained that Nicky had phoned an hour ago, asking him to drop by. He'd said he had something for him.

Lorraine looked more puzzled still. "Nicky? Phoned you? He couldn't have – not from home, anyway."

"It was Nicky's voice." *Was it?* Suspicion kicked in belatedly. The voice had sounded muffled. *Deliberately so?*

She invited him inside. The moment he set foot in the hallway, he sensed that strange aura of emptiness which persuaded him that he could range through every room, each nook and cranny, and still find no-one, because there was no-one to be found.

"He couldn't have phoned you," Lorraine pointed out patiently. "You see, he travelled up to London with me this morning by train. A meeting with his agent which usually takes the form of a late and very long lunch. I'm not expecting him back until eight or nine."

The hoaxes were coming thick and fast too. Blore apologised: obviously he'd been mistaken – some sort of practical joke. *If only.* Because he felt uncomfortable about it and could tell she'd recognised that.

She offered him tea but he declined, said he'd better get back home. Lorraine nodded sympathetically, and again he knew she'd sensed his urgency.

And urgency was putting it mildly. It would have been an ideal opportunity to raise the perfume issue, Chas's burglary, but he was too preoccupied. *Why had someone dragged him out to the other side of Didcot? And more importantly, who could it have been?*

He didn't come up with a satisfactory answer but had plenty of time for reflection. The A34, typically for the rush hour, was slow and, knowing the drive across Witney would be another nose-to-tail experience, he circumnavigated the town on country lanes. All told, the diversion to Songrise and back had taken him close on two hours.

Dusk was falling as he eased the car through his gateway. To his surprise, Whitlow's Escort was parked there, and he wondered to what he owed the pleasure. But where was Whitlow? A glance towards the house told Blore that it was in darkness.

He got out of the car and walked over to the Escort, wondered if Chas might have fallen asleep or passed out for some reason. He was nowhere in sight.

Blore's thoughts went back to the hoax, and the suspicion that something might be wrong immediately put him on the alert. He made his way down to the house, fingering the door key in his pocket. He didn't need it: the door swung open at his touch.

"Chas?" His voice trailed feebly away down the gloomy hallway. He waited but nothing came back, and as he stepped through the doorway the silence felt eerie, the landing at the top of the stairs engulfed in darkness.

Blore walked past the staircase and into the lounge. The curtains were open, so some vestige of light remained, enough to enable him to see that everything appeared to be in place.

Except that the sideboard door hung open. He wondered if he'd left it like that; and anyway at times it didn't close properly. And it could well have been that he'd forgotten to drop the catch on the front door on his way out that afternoon: after all, he'd left in a hurry, eager for Ned's news.

But he knew right away that he was kidding himself. And besides, there was the matter of Whitlow. In the next instant that one was answered, as his gaze raked the room and lit upon a pair of feet sticking out from behind the sofa.

He approached tentatively. "Chas?" Again no reply, but none was needed, for it was indeed Chas, stretched out face down, one arm out-flung and the other pinned beneath him. One of Mum's flower vases lay around in shards, and Blore, crouching, reached out a reluctant hand to find the back of Whitlow's head sticky with blood. He saw then, for his view had been obscured by the sofa, that two of the sideboard drawers hung open, their contents strewn on the floor around where Chas lay.

And then he sensed a presence in the room, heard a soft footfall behind him. He scrambled up quickly, later reflecting that that knee-jerk reaction had saved his life. Something smacked on to his shoulder, striking a glancing blow to his head on its way down. Another vase – *Christ, Mum, how many did you have?* – exploding spectacularly as it hit him, fragments flying in all directions. It was enough to send him down, but because the blow hadn't connected cleanly he didn't give way to unconsciousness, and as a bonus succeeded in cushioning the fall with his hands.

The room turned grey, the movements greyer against its background. He was aware of a third person, his attacker, in the room, rushing here, there and everywhere with manic purpose. He launched himself in the direction of where he thought the figure was and received a savage kick in the chest for his trouble. He rolled over again, bashing his head on what must have been the coffee table, fought, fought against the fading of his senses.

Blore guessed he couldn't have been out for more than seconds. He could hear no movement now, and as his eyes snapped open he was confronted by Chas: Chas prostrate, eyes closed, a feeble groan emanating from somewhere deep inside him.

And then he smelled smoke. He must have left something too close to the fire. It was starting to singe.

Wait...

There hadn't been a fire.

But undeniably there was smoke. And as any idiot knows, there's no smoke without ...

He saw it then. The only light in the house, an orange glow chasing tall, angry shadows up the walls. He raised himself on to his elbows, his head thundering. There'd been some books on the dresser, a few ancient cookery books, a couple of last week's newspapers. They were alight, the flames gradually taking hold.

Thanks to his store management responsibilities, Blore had learned enough about fire hazards to know that when the sofa and chairs caught hold, something which would happen very shortly, they'd go up within seconds, their smoke black, poisonous, deadly. There would be no escape.

He persuaded himself awake. Life – or death? *So life, suddenly and after so long, was that important again?* Oh, dear

Jesus, yes it was, precious beyond all price. No way was he ready to jack it all in yet, no way. He wanted to *live*.

Shocking himself into action, Blore struggled to his feet, thanking the God whom he'd always prevented from meaning too much to him, that the blow had fallen as he'd scrambled up, that the assailant – *here was a thought: had it been the case?* – was so much shorter than him and so hadn't been able to carry through cleanly.

No time to dwell on that now. The flames had devoured the books, reducing them to wispy black ashes, and were licking hungrily at the skirts of his armchair. And the heat was intensifying, a relentless, blistering heat. He knew there were no more than seconds left…

Thank God, he was close to the rear window. He picked up a kitchen chair and flung it with all his wavering might, the glass shattering. *All those double-glazing salesmen, Mum, and you never took the bait. Bless you, ah, bless you.*

The old kitchen rug, blotched and rotting with every imaginable culinary stain and a few others, Blore snatched up and draped over the bottom of the frame, sucking in the crisp evening air as it wafted through the opening.

With much straining and heaving, he lifted the unconscious Chas and bundled him over the sill, himself following as the sofa yielded with a violent *whoosh!* The smoke grew blacker, denser. He found himself coughing and retching, fighting, fighting to scramble out after Chas, to draw the sweet, chilling air into his lungs. Landing on the soft earth, he struggled up again to see the lounge behind him blanketed in smoke, and flames stabbing at the clouded ceiling.

Blore heard a distant siren and a commotion of voices on the road. His nearest neighbours lived in a row of cottages three hundred yards distant, and he guessed they were on their way.

His head bursting, he dragged Chas clear and laid him down beside his car, arranging him on his side so that he wouldn't swallow his tongue. It was only then that he realised that Chas was clutching something in the hand on which he'd been lying: something which looked like a square of card.

As he knelt on the stony ground, Blore's head began to whirl, and he felt his senses departing. His clothes and hair were singed, but these were the least of his worries. He thought of the house being consumed by fire, possessions of which Mum had been proud, items she'd inherited from Gran and a few – expendable – of his own.

Collapsing beside Whitlow, it occurred to him that Anita's photograph was still on the sideboard. It was all he'd had left of her and as, finally, he slipped into unconsciousness, his last thought was that its loss promised a new and strange kind of freedom.

16

Blore awoke the next morning in hospital. To begin with, he couldn't work out where he was. Once he'd come to terms with that, he took a lot longer still to work out how he came to be there.

The image of Chas floated back to him, Chas out for the count on the lounge floor, with shards of Mum's vase scattered around him. He thought back over the assault on himself, another vase, and the blow not connecting as well as had been intended.

He thanked God there and then that he hadn't been knocked unconscious. He recalled the stench of smoke, the sight of the flames, their long, deadly shadows scaling the walls; the window, mercifully, shattering and he hauling Chas out over the sill. And then oblivion.

He thought back further still to the hoax call which had taken him to Nicky Royce's house. Someone had wanted him away from home in order to lure Chas there.

But why? It didn't make sense. Why lure *Chas* to *Blore's* house? Or had Chas, for some reason, gone there of his own accord and been followed?

And had the hoax caller *known* that he'd go there, which was why he'd got Blore out of the way?

Either way Blore had arrived back a little too early and earned himself an invitation to the party. He puzzled over who it might have been, but couldn't come up with an identity to fit someone so desperate and ruthless.

A doctor looked in, gave him the once-over and said they'd keep him in for a second night, mainly for observation. He'd got off lightly, just minor burns and smoke inhalation. Blore asked about Chas.

"Well, Mr Whitlow wouldn't have been here at all if it hadn't been for you. The firemen managed to save the house, but the lounge was gutted and they'd never have got to him in time. He stands a chance, certainly. But, as I expect you know, he has a heart condition. Added to which he's in poor shape, and the nasty head wound has done him no favours."

The doctor added that the police were treating the case as arson and attempted murder. Blore had guessed that. Also they'd want to speak to him later. A Detective Inspector McCallum had been in touch. He'd guessed that too.

Into the afternoon a nurse came in, looking concerned. "Mr Blore, Mr Whitlow's asking to see you. He's lost a lot of blood and is very weak. He's beginning to get agitated. He gave me this and begged me to bring it along straight away; said you'd know what it meant. Also if you wouldn't mind seeing him in a while, I think it might help set his mind at rest."

Blore replied that he'd see Chas as soon as they liked and took the square of card the nurse held out to him. He immediately recognised it as the item Whitlow had been clutching to his chest as he'd bundled him out of the burning lounge.

It was a photograph, and right away he identified the subject. There was an inscription on the back. He read it and was left speechless. This was something he hadn't allowed for; something which wouldn't have occurred to him in a month of Sundays.

But there it was in black and white: an unassailable fact. And when, finally, he persuaded himself to believe it, a lot of things started to slot into place. And there was the hair, of course. Yes, the *hair*. Why hadn't it occurred to him sooner? He recalled – good Lord, had it only been the previous day? – Ramsey/Grayston with the long, greasy hair obscuring his face, trying to avoid being recognised.

He knew what had happened; couldn't understand why, but he *knew*. And he understood that there could be one person alone responsible for the fire, for the attempted murders of Whitlow and himself.

The nurse took him to a side ward where Chas lay propped on several pillows. His head was swathed in a turban-like bandage and, although his face bore no legacy of the fire, Blore was shocked by the sight of him. He lay there grey and shrivelled, aged by twenty years, his breathing shallow and irregular.

The nurse installed Blore in a chair beside the bed and discreetly withdrew. Chas's hand snaked out from beneath the blanket and grasped his. "You got it?" he wheezed. Blore nodded, knowing what he meant. "So you know who it was – the fire?"

"I think I've managed to work it out – guesswork for the most part."

Whitlow nodded, his lips parting in a weary smile. Clinging to Blore's hand, he started to speak. Blore tried to stop him: he needed to rest – they could talk later.

Chas shook his head. "They know there's no hope. I can see it in their faces. It was too much for the old ticker, and I can almost feel life draining out of me. Bless you, Jerry lad. All that effort to save this grouchy old bastard's life. Don't think I'm not grateful to you. But I'm on my way out, I know it for sure, and that's why I want you to know this. Listen, 'cos there's not much time."

He told Blore a story, slowly, haltingly, his voice at times sinking to a whisper, so that Blore had to strain to hear him. Once he'd finished he seemed more at ease, as if a vast burden had been lifted.

But another remained.

Whitlow hadn't relaxed his grip on Blore's hand. Now it grew tighter.

"Once I'd persuaded myself to tag along with you, I knew what I was going to do. And in the end I never did it, never got it right. So I'm sorry, Jerry, sorry for stringing you along. If there's any way you can forgive me, it'll just – well, make the going easier…"

Wasn't he the one who should have been asking forgiveness? The annoying murmur that wouldn't go away, wouldn't take no for an answer; the self-styled seeker after justice, the setter-in-train of so many unforeseen things?

Whatever. Because if he knew nothing else, Blore knew that all that had been done, all the justice that had and hadn't been meted out, that none of it could matter now. That now, finally, it was all over. His cup which had overflowed with bitterness, self-loathing and an urge for absolution had run dry.

These thoughts rattled like an express train through his mind, so that to Whitlow it must have seemed there was scarcely a pause between question and answer.

"Of course I forgive you, Chas. You didn't have to ask."

The pressure on Blore's hand relaxed, and Chas sank back on to the pillow with a sigh.

"Bless you, lad. I took a wrong turn and I'm sorry now. Straws in the wind, aren't we? Blown here, there and everywhere. Tell me, Jerry, where can we ever find that place to stop and think, and maybe retrace our steps and undo some of the wrong we've done?"

Perhaps because at various times that day he'd thought about them all, the image of Ginny Duggan sprang to mind: her faith, humility and serenity. Was that plain, undecorated avenue of sanity the one we all needed to take? Because too often we strayed down the others, blinded by their brightness, the appeal of their quick and glamorous rewards: those avenues of insanity. Blore had been that way himself and was only now clawing his way

213

back: dazzled by its lustre, heart-sickened by its reality, its visions of a living hell.

"It's so easy for us to make wrong choices," he replied. "We're all so vulnerable, even when we think we aren't."

"Just that we are what we are," Chas whispered. "And love can make kings or fools of us all."

He lapsed exhausted into a fitful sleep, and now it was Blore who clung fast to his hand. Tears wriggled down his face. He didn't try to stem them, for they were a token of his compassion, his love for an otherwise good, essentially decent man who'd made a wrong choice and wouldn't get a chance on this earth to make amends.

As time wore on, the hand in his grasp felt limp, and Blore sensed that Chas was setting out upon his final journey.

As he slipped away, his lips twitched in a fleeting, private smile. Did he see her beyond that long grey passageway of death? Was she waiting for him along the way?

For it was her name which passed almost soundlessly from his lips as he gasped his final breath:

"*Stevie.*"

17

DI McCallum was a busy woman. At least that's how Blore understood it, because she sent a young detective constable along to take his statement the following morning. Either that or he didn't rate too highly on her list of priorities, which seemed more likely.

He was discharged later that day, moving into a small bed-and-breakfast on the edge of Witney, while the insurance company arranged a short let for him. Mum's house had suffered badly in the fire, and a lot of rebuilding would have to be carried out. Blore knew right away that he could never go back there. There were too many memories, and they all rushed in upon him at once. When they'd finished with him, two images were left, superimposed indelibly upon the backcloth of the rest: Anita and Chas. He told himself they were part of the past, and that he'd lived and breathed the past for too long. He couldn't stay there, didn't wish to. Time to move on.

While he was at the b-and-b he had a visitor: McCallum. He'd guessed she'd come round to him eventually, if only out of courtesy. She was gracious and a little subdued. He wondered if she had Whitlow on her conscience, but there was no way she could have foreseen the turn events had taken.

They sat in the lounge sipping tea as the inspector apologised for not having called sooner. She assured him she'd been busy on his behalf in the meantime, investigating the cause of the fire.

"You were right, Mr Blore. Your inquiries actually accomplished more than rattling a few cages. But first off we should set a couple of issues to rest. Bobby Duggan. You state that he assaulted you outside your house the night before the fire. Mrs Royce's arrival interrupted him and he left in a hurry, although she says that she was unable to identify him.

"However, he wasn't the arsonist. That day he was working in the garden of a large house out Newbury way. He didn't leave until five. His mother states that he arrived home at a quarter-to-six, then showered and changed. At quarter-past, about the time of the fire, they were sitting down to their evening meal. If you believe Mrs Duggan – and there's no reason not to – he's in the clear."

Blore went along with that. Bobby had been passionate in his efforts to persuade him and Chas to give up the case. His methods had been far from refined, but Blore had come to understand how much Bobby's father had meant to him. He knew only too well from his own experience the pain inflicted by reopening so many old wounds. And it was only right that he'd decided not to press charges against Bobby.

"And then there's another issue," McCallum went on. "When you dragged Chas clear, he was clutching something to his chest. A nurse handed it to you at the hospital at Chas's request, and you passed it on to my colleague when he took your statement."

"Ah. The photograph."

"It opened a number of doors, didn't it, Mr Blore? A photograph of Stephanie Royce, taken before she met Nicky. The inscription on the back read: *'From Stephanie to my darling Charles, April 1963'.*" McCallum grinned ruefully. "This is why it's taken me so long to get back to you. I've been deep in the past, unearthing issues which none of us could even have suspected.

"Back in the early 1960s, Chas and Stephanie Gray, as she then was, were an item. She was the girl who ditched him. He occasionally alluded to it, but never mentioned her by name. It was a rejection which cut deep: he never got over it. He blamed Nicky Royce, the man who, in his eyes, had stolen her from him."

"But how do you know all this?"

The inspector smiled wryly. "As the result of a lot of phone calls, e-mails and questions, Mr Blore. And from the accumulation of facts. It's facts I deal in, remember, not suppositions."

He supposed he deserved the put-down but didn't retaliate. In truth he was beyond that. Chas's death had knocked a lot of the fight out of him; fight which, he now realised, had only been skin deep. He nodded for

McCallum to continue, although her next words pulled him up short.

"Chas was blackmailing Nicky Royce."

"He was doing *what*?"

"I had a long interview with Lorraine Royce. I hasten to add that *she* came to see *me*. Nicky was ill anyway, but she knew something else was getting to him, more persistent and painful than the cancer. Her first reaction was to put it down to you and your questions, although he'd seemed easy enough answering them. Then it dawned upon her that it was Chas who was giving him grief. Apparently when you visited them, Chas and Nicky disappeared for a short while?"

"Chas asked to use the loo, and Nicky showed him the way. They weren't gone long."

"They didn't need to be. Chas was quick to drop the bombshell. He'd been clearing out a cupboard a couple of days before and had come across Stephanie's photograph. He might have let it go at that, but in the next breath along you came to dig up the past, reminding him how Nicky had flourished in the years between. Chas hadn't, and he resented it. He threatened to feed the story to a muck-raking journalist: someone he could count on to blow Nicky's squeaky-clean image sky high. It would do untold damage."

"And Nicky paid up?"

McCallum shook her head. "It wasn't money Chas wanted. The threat was enough. He simply wanted Royce to suffer – payback time for some of the grief he believed Nicky had caused him."

Blore took the point. He wondered if the journalist Chas had had in mind had been Ned Hargreaves. Untold damage would have summed it up. Ned was so full of spite he'd have made life unbearable for Royce.

"The day Lorraine managed to drag all this from Nicky was the day she decided to do something about it," McCallum continued. "Chas had shown Nicky the photograph. She set out that evening to give Chas a piece of her mind. On her way to his house, she passed a restaurant and recognised your car. Thinking she might enlist your help in talking to Chas, she went in and saw the two of you having a meal together. That's when Lorraine thought she'd try her hand at a spot of burglary. She drove on to Chas's place and broke in. Once inside, she found the photograph and made off with it, only just succeeding in giving the pair of you the slip as you returned.

"She was sure Chas would know who'd taken it. But unless he had another copy, his blackmail ploy was scuppered. However, she felt sure he'd attempt to reclaim it. So after your visit to Nicky the following day, she dropped in on you on the pretext of making an apology and secreted the photograph in a drawer of your sideboard.

"Chas arrived, found her with you and was suspicious. Lorraine admits he caught her on the hop, and she let slip that she and Nicky were due at a function that evening. Chas broke into their house while they were gone: he'd have known enough to be capable of silencing the alarm. But he didn't find what he wanted. That was when he put two and two together and decided to try your place. He got lucky. You weren't there, and he forced his way in and found what he wanted where Lorraine had hidden it.

"But he hadn't been watching his back. Someone was following him: the person who started the fire and who, in effect, was responsible for his death."

Blore had been thinking it out. "And that wasn't Bobby Duggan or Lorraine Royce. So it had to be Nicky. He didn't meet up with his agent, did he? Once he parted company with Lorraine at Paddington, he caught the next train back and drove over to shadow Chas. As soon as Chas came out to his car, Nicky phoned me and got me to head out to Songrise so that I was well out of it. I suspect Chas stopped off along the way – probably for a pint, knowing him – which explains why Royce was still at my place when I showed up." Blore let out a whistle. "When this gets out, it's going to make headlines."

McCallum smiled grimly as she shook her head. "Maybe not," she said. "Because you see, Mr Blore, the headlines have already been made. Nicky Royce took his own life yesterday. His wife found him on her return from work. A cocktail of alcohol and pills. He left a note – genuine, in case you wonder – informing her that he couldn't face the torment of a long illness. He'd decided to take a quick way out."

★★★

Blore knew nothing would come of it now, with Chas and Nicky both dead. DI McCallum was astute enough to see that it was going nowhere and compassionate enough not to press charges against Lorraine for breaking and entering.

The insurance company found him a small terraced house in the centre of Witney, which he took on a six-month let while the cottage was being rebuilt. Into December now, and he found it cosy: an open fire in the tiny living room, a postage stamp-sized back garden to potter about in, pleasant neighbours. He considered making an offer for it once he had a buyer for Mum's.

Blore attended Chas's funeral at Oxford Crematorium. It was a quiet affair, a couple of distant cousins who admitted they hadn't seen Chas in years, some ex-colleagues dour and sober-suited, Mary McCallum and himself. Blore felt sad, because he'd liked Chas, and because this tiny gathering said it all. The ex-DS, shorn of his job, had been a man with few friends and a lot of bitterness. A lonely man, shiftless; a straw in the wind. Blore could see himself heading in the same direction, and there was no way he wanted that. There had to be more to life.

By contrast Nicky Royce's funeral was getting on for a state occasion. He'd been the last and arguably the most talented of the Makeweights. A TV documentary trumpeted his achievements, a galaxy of stars paid tribute and Ned Hargreaves wormed his way on to a couple of chat shows on the pretext that his friendship with 'our dear Nick' qualified him to write the authorised biography. Inevitably a 'Greatest Hits' volume was released, with the unspoken promise of one every two years for the foreseeable, a film of his life was promised, and a plethora of obituaries poured forth, fulsome in their praise.

But to Blore it all felt no less sad than Chas's passing. No real friends, no less bitterness. Another straw in the wind. The words Nicky had penned for one of the group's monster hits might have been prophetic:

> *Don't start now,*
> *I'm not in this place.*
> *I'm stealing on the breeze*
> *With everything you owned.*
> *Your weeping after me*
> *Won't bring me back.*
> *I'm gone, I'm long time gone,*
> *So don't start now.*

He phoned Lorraine before the funeral. No way he intended to go, for he believed he had no place there, but he wanted to offer his condolences and expected to get short shrift. He began to stutter the customary Blore-like apologies, but she interrupted him.

"It wasn't your fault, Jerry."

"I got Chas Whitlow interested in this."

"But you weren't to know he had his own agenda. I suspected at first that you might be in it with him and quickly decided that you weren't. And you didn't come out of it exactly unscathed yourself. I heard you were in hospital. How are things now?"

Touched by her concern, he told her he was fine, but that the house had fared badly. She asked him where he was staying and he told her, adding that its anonymity suited him, that he was determined to sell the cottage once it was habitable.

"That's something we've got in common, then," she replied. "Because I shan't be staying here. Nicky left me the house, but I've never felt I belonged here. It was hers – Stephanie's. Anyway, I'm not likely to have the time to look after a place this size. Lynne, my business associate, has asked me to return to work full-time. She's looking to open a couple of new outlets: Oxford and Reading. So there'll be plenty for me to get on with. In the meantime I shall be clearing up Nicky's effects. Ginny Duggan has offered to help, so I shan't be lonely."

Blore decided to sign off there and wished her a peaceful Christmas.

"You too, Jerry. Mine'll be quiet, and I welcome that. I shall be with my parents on the south coast. Then it's back here, put the house on the market and hope for a quick sale."

She sounded upbeat. But he'd never had the impression that she'd be one to mope. Nicky's illness had probably prepared her for the worst, and she'd always struck Blore as one who was all for getting on with her life.

★★★

Not long before Christmas, DI McCallum visited him again, this time bearing gifts. Her team had searched Chas's house, looking for clues to tie him in to the blackmail of Nicky Royce. Royce's suicide, just a few days later, had rendered the operation redundant, but they'd come across a journal written during the late summer and early autumn.

It illustrated the way Chas's mind had been working. And right after that Blore had happened along, the catalyst sparking it all into life. There was, of course, no way he could have known that; but he wished he hadn't. If things had been different, if he hadn't been a recovering drunk with something to prove in his sad life. If…if…if…

We are what we are. Those had been almost Chas's last words to him. He heard him again, uttering them in a dying whisper as he fought for breath.

Regret it as he might, the damage was done, with no way of going back. Only of going on.

Blore sat and pored over the journal. He had, after all, few Christmas cards to send and no presents to buy.

It didn't take a lot of studying: they were random thoughts in which Chas's hurt and resentment were evident. But Blore, with time on his hands, gave the matter extensive thought and set down a few ideas of his own. There didn't seem a lot in what Whitlow said; but a whole lot more in what he didn't say.

I found her photograph today…stared into the face which even now is snapping at the frontier of my dreams. I felt the old wounds reopening, and perhaps I shouldn't have been surprised…Because none of them have ever healed.

I was left to pick up the pieces of my life. And as I look back down the years, I realise that's all there have ever been: pieces.

So I waited, because I was sure she'd leave him soon…It would dawn upon her how much I had loved her and that she could depend on me…And I waited, waited. But she never returned.

I've given this weeks of thought: painful, grinding weeks…And the residue is bitterness. I know now and at last what I didn't know before. And I'm determined to make him pay.

Blore hardly noticed Christmas: it came and went, despite the insistent bells beckoning him to church. He didn't go. But what he did was something he hadn't done since his far-off schooldays, when attendances at church services at Christmas, Easter and on Ascension Day had been compulsory. He prayed.

He prayed for them all: Anita and Cassie, his lost loves; for Chas, Nicky and Lorraine, Ginny and Bobby; and for purpose and direction for himself in the days ahead. It felt strange, praying. He couldn't be sure anyone was listening. But he hoped someone was.

On New Year's Eve he took himself off for a long walk. It was the prelude to the Millenium, a new century. Everyone's mood seemed buoyant, and drinking and partying had started early. He was back indoors before it got into full swing.

Blore trawled back over the notes he'd made. He wondered about running them past McCallum. *With my caseload?* She'd dismiss them as speculation, and in any case most of the *dramatis personae* were dead.

Yet, oddly for Blore, it wasn't all doom and gloom. New Year's Eve: the threshold of a new beginning. If this had been a film or book, it would end with the tear-inducing neatness of Cassie knocking on his door at midnight, begging for the chance to come back into his life. Some chance. Before Christmas he'd placed his temporary address and mobile number in the personal column of a couple of the magazines she used to read. Just in case. And anyway, when all was said and done, he was the one who should do the begging.

It was well into the evening when the knock sounded at the door. It didn't register with him at first, deep in the diversion of an inane TV show. When it did, he catapulted out of his chair and raced for the front door, his heart pounding with impossible expectation.

Lorraine Royce stood before him, swathed in thick woolly scarf and long black coat. She looked fragile and uncertain, more so the longer he stared at her as if he'd never seen her before.

"Jerry. I – I'm sorry. Look, if it's not convenient, I'll -."

"No. It's fine. Please – please come in."

He held the door, and she stepped past him into the living room.

"This is cosy."

The fire was roaring, the room so cramped it couldn't hold much more than the two of them, but comfortable and warm.

"I like it."

"But if I'm intruding in any way? If you just wanted to be alone?"

"You're not, and I don't. Although I don't know what sort of company I'll be. As you'd probably guess, I'm not the partying type."

She smiled, seemed more relaxed now. "Me neither. There were invitations – people have been very kind. But tonight, well, I just didn't feel I could." She looked round the room. "I nearly didn't come here. It was only as I parked up the road that I wondered if perhaps your wife - ?"

Blore shook his head. "I've been wondering too. But I'm certain she won't come. Here, let me take your coat and scarf. I'll put the kettle on. I think there's some shortbread biscuits too." He grinned. "As you can see, I'm going flat out to welcome the Millenium."

He took her things and hung them on the back of the door, went through to the kitchen and filled the kettle. She followed him. She hadn't handed over her shoulder bag and now she was taking a plain buff folder from it. Once more her manner was hesitant.

"The reason I called was to bring you this. I think you should read it. And this time it's I who've come to you with an apology. Because, Jerry, you were right all along. Anita Mead didn't kill Boyd Neelan."

Blore was amazed at his own calmness as he clicked the kettle switch and turned slowly to face her.

"I know," he said. "Because Stevie did."

18

In the end Lorraine made the tea, put the biscuits on a plate and brought the tray into the living room. Blore had his head deep in the manuscript he'd pulled from the folder. He was busy being justified. Over the past days, since he'd left hospital and had time on his hands, time to walk and ponder, there'd been several scenarios buzzing around in his head, all of them pure speculation but yelling at him that the killer hadn't been Anita after all.

And then there'd been Chas. Chas had been the key and, going by what he'd been so desperate to avoid saying, Blore had known that it had had to be Stevie.

I met Stevie during the summer of 1963. It was before Phil and I formed the Makeweights. We were playing at a dance at a village hall somewhere out near Wantage. By the middle of our act, I was conscious of this girl at the edge of the stage, jigging along to the beat. There was a guy with her, and they were arguing. Finally she turned her back on him and he went away. She stayed. I was concentrating on the act but was alive to the fact that she didn't take her eyes off me.

When it was time for us to take a break, I sought her out. The guys were joshing me about her, but I shrugged them off. Phil and Ginny were practically married anyway, and the other lads – I can't even remember their names, but the group split with the birth of the Makeweights – had steady girls. I'd always been the loner, hitched up to my music.

But soon I had my girl too. I bought her a drink, and we sat and chatted a while. Her name was Stephanie, but she preferred to be called Stevie. She was attractive: in no way could she be described as beautiful, but she had such *presence* and was so full of – what shall I call it? – vim, get-up-and-go. I'd never met anyone so vital, so utterly dedicated to living.

The guy she'd been with came back. She walked to the door with him, deep in conversation, and sent him on his way. She never told me his name, simply referred to him as 'my ex'. Apparently he'd wanted to punch me on the nose, but she persuaded him to go home and cool off. She liked the music and was staying. She told me he wasn't a fan of pop music and hadn't wanted to come along anyway.

At the end of the gig she came home with me. I shared a flat with Phil and Ginny and took a lot of ragging from Phil and the other lads. I didn't care. It may not have taken me long, but I knew I was head over heels in love.

By spring of the following year, we'd married. Phil and Ginny were wed too, and on the music front we'd found a couple of decent session men and were looking to take a step up. All we needed was a name. Stevie came up with the Makeweights, because she reckoned she and Ginny were the movers and shakers. In her opinion, Phil and I were too laid back for our own good, simply content to let things happen around us.

But the Makeweights were no joke. I'd always been a song-writer first and performer second. If I say it myself, though, I'd always played a decent lead guitar and could handle vocals okay as long as the lyrics were mine.

That's another part of the effect Stevie had on me. I wrote songs like a man possessed. Well, I think that's what I was: possessed – by *her*. She *drove* me, became my reason for living.

Then Boyd came along. I knew Ned Hargreaves from way back, always with an eye for the main chance. He liked our songs, offered to be our manager, sort out the gigs for us. But he reckoned we'd only go places with the right front man. With Ned you either love him or hate him. Mainly hate him, I guess, but in this instance he was spot on. He'd 'discovered' Boyd Neelan in some poxy little night club and asked Phil and I to give him a try-out as a vocalist. Boyd had something: charisma, perhaps, rather than presence. He came to us as a gangling twenty year-old with fuzz on his face, pimply and awkward in an ill-fitting hand-me-down suit and down-at-heel winkle-pickers.

But, man, could he sing. Like, really belt out the words. We cut a demo, and after a few months got our big chance. The song was *Crazy Heart*. Stevie and I had had a spat over nothing, and before I apologised – I always apologised because I felt so wretched – I wrote the song in ten minutes flat. We made it on to *Juke Box Jury*. The jury voted it a hit, and they weren't wrong. Then *Ready, Steady, Go*. That was the clincher. Well, that and Ned insisting we rename the group Boyd Neelan and the Makeweights.

You've no idea how Stevie kicked up about that. It was *my* song, and the group was mine and Phil's. She ripped Ned to shreds over it, scared the poor little sod out of his wits. At one point I thought she was going to kill him. As for Boyd, she nearly had him in tears, apologising for all he was worth. In the end I said we'd give it a try, see how it worked out. It was still my song, and if we were to go places it could only be as a group, all the talents gelling together. Stevie wasn't happy, but it was a question of live with it or cancel *RSG*. And if we'd done that, we'd never have been asked again.

Of course, on *RSG* you had to mime. Boyd was a revelation. He seized the moment, performing in front of the Makeweights' biggest audience to date. Without doubt a star in the making.

You take my world
and turn it upside down,
and all the time
you got me spinning round.
Maybe it's true
We oughta stay apart,
But I can't let you go –

It's just my crazy heart.

Hearts were what he won over. Ginny had to take on the role of fan club secretary, because we were inundated with letters to Boyd saying, like, how could that bitch be so cruel to *you*, you're just *fab*, and here's my address and photograph and I don't have a boyfriend at the moment.

We hit number two within three weeks. Only the Beatles kept us off the top. It was our first gold disc. The first LP was only a month away, and the hits kept coming. We couldn't believe it. Even Ned was knocked for six.

Well, as I say, it was the group's success. But Boyd was the front man, the linchpin. Without him we wouldn't have enjoyed anywhere near the success we did. Okay, they were mostly my songs we used, although Boyd and I had started to collaborate: he'd write some lyrics, and I'd stick in a middle eight, tidy it up and round it off. Well, anyone else might have used the songs I wrote back then. But only Boyd could bring them to life.

And as he did, he started to grow bigger than the group. Phil and Ginny didn't seem to mind, and it didn't bother me a lot because I was getting to write my songs, and because Boyd and I got along well. I was a few years older than him and knew the score. I suppose I saw myself as his mentor.

But Stevie hated him. She told me so. She said that from the first night we'd met she'd seen I was a talented guy, felt I could go places with my songs, and she was behind me all the way. She felt bitter about the fact that it was she who'd suggested the group's name, and now that was all we'd become: makeweights.

Boyd tried hard with Stevie, but it was only for my sake she tolerated him, and then barely. Of course as the money rolled in, so did the women. Hargreaves engineered his marriage to Suzy Steller. It was fantastic publicity – all three of them saw it that way. I swear there wasn't an ounce of love in that union, unless it was self-love. From the off, Boyd and Suzy were in direct competition to see who could become the biggest star. The year she hit the number one spot with that inane Christmas song, Boyd went ape. Man, he was sick for weeks, and it didn't help matters between him and Suzy.

They'd bought Dreamfields together, but Suzy hardly set foot in it, preferring the London scene. And with her out of the way, Boyd brought in girl after girl. Sometimes they'd last a week, maybe two; seldom much longer. Stevie and I lived more modestly down the road in Chelfold. I'd wanted to be near Boyd, because he'd had a studio built at Dreamfields and we used it to write and rehearse our songs. Looking back, I wished we'd moved miles away. If we had, Boyd Neelan might still be alive today.

It's been well documented that Boyd was insatiable where women were concerned. Anyone was fair game. He tried his luck with Ginny Duggan, which just went to show that he did all his thinking below the belt. Because if there was any woman determined to stay faithful to her man, that woman would be Ginny.

Then he turned his attention to Stevie. He'd always flirt outrageously, and both Ginny and Stevie would give it back. It was no more than a bit of fun on their part, but I soon saw that Boyd was attracted to Stevie.

He was devious about it, always waiting until I was off the scene. Then he'd come on to her big-time. One evening I got back home to find her in tears. I believe that was the first time I'd ever seen her so helpless. It took me a long while to drag the truth from her. That afternoon Boyd had lured her over to Dreamfields and raped her.

I was beside myself with fury. I'd always been a mild sort of guy, and I shocked her with my threats of vengeance. I stalked to the door, intending to drive over there right away and have it out with him. I know I'd made up my mind to kill him.

Stevie hauled me back, reasoned with me, told me not to be a fool. She begged me to say and do nothing. It took some time, but eventually she won me round.

Things calmed down for a while, but then to our mutual horror Stevie and I found that relations between us had become strained. He'd come between us, driven a wedge through the heart of our marriage; and it was as if, too, he'd driven it under our skins, so that nothing in our lives was or could ever be the same again. At least not while he lived.

Again Stevie was the voice of reason. Boyd had treated her badly, but he'd treated me worse, flying in the face of our friendship. She asked me to let her give the matter some thought. She'd work something out: we'd get even with him.

Boyd, meanwhile, continued on his merry way as if nothing at all had happened. I maintained the appearance of friendship, but beneath it I was seething. I loathed him and could hardly wait for the opportunity to punish him.

His latest girlfriend was Anita Mead, dizzy and biddable, an attractive girl with a mane of corn-blonde hair. Stevie had no time for Boyd's women, and for several weeks had been contemplating how we might be able to use Anita to our advantage. I don't know what Boyd had promised the girl, but she believed everything he said and gave herself airs, obviously envisaging herself as mistress-in-waiting of Dreamfields.

It didn't alarm me that Stevie had been thinking along these lines. My initial rage had subsided, but we'd been hurt and the wound had festered in us both. The revenge on Boyd was always going to have to be final, and if the girl's death was necessary for us to achieve that goal, then so be it.

Boyd's ideas, booze- and acid-induced, seemed to get wilder by the day. He was angling to replace Phil Duggan with Sonny Ralston, a totally unsuitable choice. I told Stevie I wasn't going to let it happen. She said not to worry: it wouldn't.

She'd learned from Ginny that on the coming Saturday Phil had arranged to meet Boyd in the studio at eleven a.m. She took that as our starting point, because Phil was always punctual to the second.

I arranged to spend the first part of that morning in the studio with Boyd. There were problems with a song he'd been writing, and he needed my help. He was agitated, because he didn't want me to find out about the impending interview with Phil – guilt kicking in, I expect. If he'd had anything resembling a brain, he'd have known that Phil would have already informed me about it. Anita was there, preparing Boyd's habitual early lunch. We'd carefully noted her outfit: a red-and-white hooped mini dress and white calf-length boots. Over the previous weeks, Stevie had purchased a number of outfits identical to those favoured by Anita.

Boyd decided he'd had enough, and I was dismissed. It was just after half-past ten. I stuck my head round the kitchen door and asked Anita if I could have a word outside. She followed me out.

Then something happened which we couldn't have foreseen. Suzy Steller came roaring up the drive in her yellow sports job, effing and blinding like a fishwife. Anita fled, disappearing off into the shrubbery. That wasn't meant to happen.

But Stevie, as I might have known, had a back-up plan. She was waiting there for Anita and overpowered her. We put her in the boot of my car. As Suzy left, Stevie ensured that she glimpsed her, dressed identically to Anita and with a blonde wig over her own hair. Seen in passing, she *was* Anita.

I drove home. I'd only just got there when Suzy roared past on her way back through the village. With her out of the way, Stevie went into the studio, dealt with Boyd and came running out as Phil and Bobby arrived. Boyd's blood was on the knife and on her hands. She dropped the knife, took Boyd's Mustang and wiped her hands on the rug in the car.

She'd thought of everything. The knife was from the studio kitchen and as such already had Anita's fingerprints on it. Stevie wrapped a handkerchief round the top of the handle so that her prints wouldn't get on it, and Anita's for the main part remained intact.

She left the car at Didcot station, taking care to wipe her prints off the steering wheel with the bloodstained rug. As anticipated, concealed among so many, it was a while before the police found the car. She caught a train to Mardon Regis. In that bright dress and with the big blonde hair, she knew someone was bound to notice her along the way. But she made every effort to keep as low a profile as possible, because her work was nowhere near finished.

Once in Mardon, she booked into Seabirds. It wasn't a random choice: it had been chosen because it was a bungalow and close to the sea-front. She booked in as 'Susan Starr' – a deliberate swipe at Suzy – and in the early evening, having changed her clothes and removed the wig, she left Seabirds via her bedroom window and returned to Didcot by train, her arrival coinciding with that of a London train. After all, she was supposed to have been in London all day.

I'd taken the unconscious Anita back to my place and kept her quiet there for the rest of the day. In the early hours of the next morning, with Stevie reprising the Anita role, I drove her back to Seabirds, and she re-entered her room by the way she'd left. The real Anita was back in the boot of my car. We'd kept her well subdued.

That morning Stevie and I played out a scenario for the benefit of the Seabirds landlady. I donned an Afro wig, afghan, neckerchief and loons and made myself conspicuous outside the shops opposite the guest house. Stevie 'saw' me and created a diversion so that she could slip away. I picked her up, and we drove a few miles out of town to a convenient spot where we staged Anita's suicide. We changed back into our regular clothes and returned home, where we burned the outfits we'd used that day.

I'd deliberately disguised myself along the lines of a guy I knew had been hanging round after Suzy. Along with the 'Susan Starr' alias, we felt that if the police got hooked on the Mardon angle, it would create a lot of hassle for our Miss Steller.

We accepted that it might lead to further inquiries and that we'd need to cover our tracks because we might be under scrutiny. But it never got that far. The officer in charge was under pressure from above to furnish a quick result. And it all fitted so neatly and obviously into place, particularly as there was no way Anita could plead her innocence.

★★★

So that's how it happened. I have no excuses. I am just as guilty as Stevie, and yet her coldness and calculation the whole way through alarmed me. She suggested, planned and organised it all. She *drove* it, just as she drove me.

It all blew over. The Makeweights had a massive post-Boyd sympathy hit. We cut a new album, using session men, which did pretty well. But in the words of that same hit song, Phil and I knew that without Boyd we had nowhere to go. For all his faults, he'd been the man, the catalyst, the interpreter of our combined talents.

We disbanded. Phil tried his luck with a couple of other groups, couldn't rediscover the spark and took up teaching and writing drum tutorials. I went solo for a while, couldn't – didn't really want to – make it work and earned my living writing songs for other people. Stevie and I settled back into our routine, but I was never easy in my mind again.

Sadly, I think she was. I think she felt justified by what she'd done, and she tried to erase the memory of it from both our lives. She was a greater prop to me than ever and a tremendous help in my work. We lived well, holidayed extravagantly and often, happy in each other's company. Stevie got involved in village life: the WI, village fetes, amateur dramatics. The villagers really warmed to her and, by association, me. We seemed well and truly back on track.

And then the bomb dropped.

It was Ginny's suggestion, but I think Ned Hargreaves, scenting publicity and therefore money, was at the back of it. A tribute group had already been formed, and the label was going to release another 'Greatest Hits' to celebrate the Makeweights' twentieth anniversary, even though the group had folded more than ten years previously.

Ginny and Stevie planned the whole thing. We had a villa in Spain then, and they had the idea of hiring a yacht and throwing a big party out at sea. Anyone who'd ever been associated with the group was invited. That meant including Suzy Steller and her love of the moment. I wasn't too happy about that, but if we snubbed her she'd only go running to some tame journalist, and our names would be mud.

I wasn't much in favour of the party in the first place, but Phil was in the first stages of what would prove a long illness, and I think Ginny saw it as a way of lifting him out of himself and giving us all a massive shot in the arm of nostalgia. So I decided to go along with it, although there hadn't really been a choice. For Stevie, it was a project, something to organise, and she threw herself into it wholeheartedly.

The event itself was a disaster in every way. I don't know who brought the drugs on board, but they got passed round pretty smartly, and what with enough booze to sink a fleet, practically everyone was off his or her face in no time.

Ned Hargreaves, not for the first time, tried to hit on Suzy with, for him, catastrophic results. She humiliated him in front of the whole gathering, and I doubt if he's ever forgiven her.

He'd brought along some girl whom he'd promised to get into films. You know the patter: contacts here, there and everywhere, the man in the know. I've never heard of her since. I have the feeling she'd got it into her tiny mind that all of us were something big in the film world, because she tried to hitch up to everything in trousers with, as you'd guess, the exception of poor Ned. I can't work out to this day how it came about, but she ended up in my bed. I mean, I was so completely out of my skull, and because of that I don't think anything actually happened. She left, and I must have passed out with the party reverberating around me.

When I came to, Stevie was there. She was livid, demanding to know what the hell I thought I was playing at. We'd been together twenty years, and I'd never been unfaithful to her.

She was drunk – who wasn't? – but ice-cold and utterly in control. I tried to calm her down, to reason with her, but she wouldn't listen.

She told me with exaggerated composure that that afternoon twelve years before, when she'd claimed Boyd had raped her, she'd not been speaking the truth. They'd made love. She'd given herself to him willingly. He'd wanted for them to be an item, because he knew she could inspire and motivate him in the same way she'd done for me. And she'd been sorely tempted.

But she'd agreed to nothing. Because she soon realised that she'd been an utter fool. She'd fallen for that tried and trusted Neelan charm, the way a stupid chit of a girl like Anita had. And all he'd wanted had been to get her into bed: that was about as far as Boyd's agenda ever went.

In doing so, he signed his death warrant. Because he held the trump card and, loose cannon that he was, would be liable to use it at any time, boasting aloud that he'd screwed his best friend's wife. Stevie had been insulted, and from that moment had started to plot the ultimate revenge. And she'd carried it out with me, the cuckolded husband, as her willing conspirator.

241

She told me this and paused, staring down at me in a superior manner. Top that, she seemed to be saying, top that with your grubby, drunken little fumblings in the dark.

I got off the bed. My head was thundering, and I put my hands over my eyes. And then I hit her.

It was the last thing she'd expected. She gasped, stared at me wide-eyed, a large red weal across her cheek. She started to speak, but I didn't give her the chance. I hit her again, full-bloodedly this time with my fist. The force of it lifted her off her feet and set her staggering backwards. She fell awkwardly, striking her head on the edge of a table as she went down. She sat slumped in the corner of the room, staring at me dazedly.

It was only when she didn't move at all that I realised I'd killed her. I felt desperately and in vain for a pulse. I panicked. I don't know how much I'd drunk, but I was suddenly stone-cold sober. Surely she couldn't be *dead?* I tried for a pulse again. Nothing. In the end, knowing I couldn't let her be discovered there in the cabin, my anxiety got the better of me. I picked her up, stumbled outside and, after ensuring that no-one was in the vicinity, pitched her over the rail and into the sea.

I went back in, tidied the cabin and washed my face. Then I staggered back to the party and raised the alarm. We searched everywhere for her, alerted the police and coastguard. Her body was washed ashore the next morning.

The police gave us all, especially me, an almighty grilling. I don't know how I managed to hold up to question after question, but somehow I got through, and the conclusion was drawn that she'd gone overboard owing to the excesses of the party. Several of our number had noticed that she'd been drinking heavily.

I didn't have to manufacture my grief, my sense of total loss. I was devastated. I don't know what had made me hit out at her. Never before had I raised a finger, nor even been so much as angry with her. Unless it was my own guilt that tore away at me; that and the knowledge of her calculated infidelity, the fact that I'd come so close to losing her. Perhaps Boyd had been deadly serious after all, and she hadn't seen it. I ached for the opportunity to look her in the eyes and forgive her, beg her forgiveness and go back to where we'd been before.

The house became her memorial, she who'd done so much to create its living, vibrant atmosphere; and it became her mausoleum. It was only you, Lori, who came along a few years later and set me on my feet again. You became my prop, even though I was never able to confess until now what's written here. Even so, I believe you felt yourself overshadowed by her. I was too, if that's any comfort. For she has never left me, always and everywhere a reminder of my guilt.

But the final destruction wasn't far away. I'd seen little of Charles Whitlow during the investigation into Boyd's murder. Stevie and I were questioned by his superior, Arnison, and Whitlow was sent to Mardon Regis to look into matters there. I've often wondered if that was at his own request. Even so, I'd recognised Whitlow as Stevie's ex, and I wondered if he'd be out to make trouble for me.

Fortunately Arnison got the quick result he'd been hoping for – it couldn't have looked more cut and dried – and I didn't see Whitlow again until he turned up on my doorstep not much more than a week ago with that guy Blore.

He drew me aside on a pretext and spoke to me. Blore's coming to see him had set him thinking, and after so many years he suddenly found himself viewing the case in a different light, certain now that the events at Mardon Regis had warranted further investigation. He told me what he thought had happened. He'd guessed right in almost every detail. And although I tried hard not to react, assuring him that it simply wasn't so, I could see that he didn't believe me.

He showed me a photograph of Stevie, taken when they'd been courting. He'd recently happened upon it. She'd inscribed it on the back, and he'd taken those words to heart, having held a torch for her all these years.

Whitlow accused me of her murder, although he didn't have a shred of proof. He suggested he might go to the papers with his story, which would blow my clean-living, respectable image sky high. I offered to come to an arrangement, but it wasn't money he wanted. He just wanted me to suffer, and he'd started the process tellingly. For once he'd gone, I was left hanging in a limbo of utter torment.

I told Lori right away. I confessed to having killed Stevie and swore it had been an accident. I couldn't bring myself to say anything about the business with Boyd.

First and foremost, Lori was appalled at the deterioration in me. The cancer was setting in, and I was due a course of chemo. Mentally I'd kept myself up to the mark, even though my body was suffering. I'd known for a while that it'd get me in the end, but in the space of those last few minutes I could tell that Whitlow had accelerated the process, and I was crumbling totally.

Lorraine took pity, and I bless her for sticking by me, for doing wrong in order to set my troubled mind at rest. She managed to retrieve the photograph. We knew he'd come looking for it, and that he would know only we could have taken it. So, unknown to Blore, Lorraine secreted it at his house. Unfortunately Whitlow showed up there unannounced as she was about to leave, and she felt sure he suspected what she'd done. Of course, he was desperate to get it back. It was the only photograph he possessed, and without it his case against me would be severely hampered.

But Lorraine had taken enough risks on my behalf. It was now down to me to achieve closure. I was certain that, having burgled our house and failed to find what he wanted, Whitlow would go to Blore's. The following day I parked down the road from him, and when he finally emerged I tailed him. I guessed where he was heading so, as added insurance, phoned Blore's mobile and sent him off on a fool's errand. I wanted it to be Whitlow and myself.

Sure enough, he made his way to Blore's house. Not as quickly as I'd hoped, because he stopped off for a drink along the way and took his time over it. Dutch courage, I suppose. Once there, he prowled around for a while, although I could have told him no-one was in. I watched him pick the lock, then went stealthily in behind him. I hit him over the head with a vase, and he collapsed.

Then I heard a car. Blore had arrived back. I cursed. Ten more minutes and I'd have been out of there. I didn't want to do what I knew was necessary. I had no particular grudge against Blore, but he was in my way. He shouldn't have been there. I came up behind, hit him and he went down. I searched around for the photograph, couldn't find it. And then I thought, *what the hell?* The madness was well and truly upon me by then; panic too, and I just wanted out of there. I set fire to the room, intending to kill them both, obliterate everything so that I'd be safe.

As I say, I was mad, not thinking straight. This wasn't me at all. I'm glad Blore got out – I owe him an apology. And even though Whitlow didn't die in the blaze, I alone am responsible for his death.

As I am responsible for my own. Lori, this confession is for you. I know it will cut you to the heart, and I'm sorry. I pray that one day you may look back on all this and find that you can forgive me. And that you will try hard always to remember me as the man you knew: a poor fool lacking utterly in self-esteem, only able to stand with the support of a good and true woman. That was what Stevie might have been. It is undoubtedly what you are.

★★★

Blore closed the folder. He looked up to find Lorraine in the seat opposite. He couldn't tell how long she'd been there, patiently waiting for him to finish, tears brimming in her eyes.

"You were right, Jerry." Her voice wavered, barely above a whisper. "Anita was innocent. You can get justice for her now."

"Then – you're giving this to me?"

"Yes. I believe you have a right to do with it as you see fit. I never want to see it again. My duty is to fulfil his last wish, because he was so good to me. That's to remember him as I knew him: a gentle, kind, helpless man who couldn't stand alone."

Blore clutched the manuscript in both hands as he reflected upon what he'd done to get this far. He wondered what he could achieve for Anita now. Justice? But who would remember her? And who, apart from himself, would care? He thought of Nicky, of Stevie and Chas. They hadn't been bad people, but they'd been carried away into doing bad things, because they'd allowed themselves to be dragged along by the world, to be instructed in its ways and dance to its deafening symphony of destruction.

We could make a killing, my friend. This could be big, big, **big**.

Echoes of little Hargreaves and his ilk rained in upon him. *Big?* Try earth-shattering, Ned. Try devastating.

He pushed them all aside, knowing that it profits a man nothing to grow rich on and glory in another's misery, capitalise upon his shame. We let the world reduce us all, when our time comes, to nothing greater or better than straws in the wind. And the world had done enough for Blore already. It was time for a line to be drawn under the sadness.

With savage deliberation he tore the manuscript in half and then again, placed the fragments on the fire and watched them burn.

"But, Jerry -!" Lorraine was on her feet, gesticulating at the fire, tears streaming down her face as she stared at him in disbelief. "It's what you've wanted, what you've been searching for. Your proof that Anita -."

"Is innocent." He looked up at her. "I know that. I may not have actually *known* it before, but I do now. And God knows. I think I'm coming to understand that's all that should ever really matter."

"Then thank you. Oh Jerry, thank you." She stumbled forward, and he rose and caught her in his arms, held her close as she sobbed out her gratitude.

Outside, the Millenium celebrations were getting under way with a vengeance. Fireworks painted the sky, and people thronged the street on their way between pubs and parties, the air vibrant with their merriment.

"A new year," Blore said. "A new century. Time for doors to close and others to open. Perhaps that *is* something to celebrate. Would you like a drink? There's only water, I'm afraid."

Lorraine smiled up at him. "Water will be fine."

He fetched some from the fridge and poured it. They raised their glasses. It was clear, cool and uncomplicated, the way he knew his life had to be. The past was gone, the last of it blackened and crumbled by the hungry flames. Long time gone, as Nicky had written and Boyd had sung. Somewhere, somehow, a future stretched before him, and he began to feel the faint stirrings of hope in his heart.